Natalie Clifford Barney

THE ONE
WHO IS LEGION

OR

A.D.'S AFTER-LIFE

THE ONE
WHO IS LEGION

Natalie Clifford Barney (1876-1972) was an American writer who spent most of her life in Paris, and formed notorious relationships with, among others, Liane de Pougy, Lucie Delarue-Mardrus, and Renée Vivien. During her lifetime she published five volumes of poetry; three of epigrams; two books of essays; and one novel, *The One Who is Legion, or AD's After-Life* (1930); as well as three memoirs.

SNUGGLY BOOKS

CONTENTS

"For Spirits when they please
Can either sex assume, or both; so soft
And uncompounded is their essence pure,
Not tied or manacled with joint or limb,
Nor founded on the brittle strength of bones,
Like cumbrous flesh; but in what shape they choose,
Dilated or condensed, bright or obscure,
Can execute their airy purposes,
And works of love or enmity fulfil."

Paradise Lost.

"Ce sera tout-à-fait comme dans cette vie."

O. W. DE MILOSZ.

THE ONE
WHO IS LEGION

Chapter I

AN ADVENTURE IN INTEGRATION

IN the Bois de Boulogne, opposite the Longchamps race-course, lies the graveyard where the nuns of Longchamps were buried after the destruction of their abbey. In the nineteenth century it gave burial to "La Guimard," and extended the hospitality of its enriched earth to many more recent guests. The dead of the romantic period had a predilection for this cemetery.

A grey breed of Andalusian hens and two ash-coloured cocks with flaming crests strut about this enclosure by day, cared for by the guardian and his wife who live there, less in fear of seeing what remains of these remains desecrated by the rapacious *Conseil Municipal*, than of having their little house given to some rustic policeman. Although there survive a few *concessionnaires* who can protect these graves, no one is sure of resting in peace, not even the dead, for even in this really dead graveyard the earth mounds and tossed headstones suggest that they are most restless and have turned in their sleep.

A triumphant vegetation of undergrowth, overgrowing everything, bends down under its supple labyrinth trees caught with their branches in tresses of bindweed; and persistent convolvulus—a snare of living twigs meshed together as nimbly as those of basket-weavers—contrives high cages for the soaring leaves.

Deep-rooted trees swell their veined grip above the ground; entwining parasites reach up over their tallest crests, then coil down again upon themselves, binding together in virulent attachments a wild lettering of forgotten names. Reptile shapes and stings are apprehended, as a switch swings aggressively back into place, or gives a bitter greensap smell in breaking. A whistle—a call for help? The bent elbow of a willow is thrown about the stone neck of a column—a leaning pillar against the trunk of the tree; stone and wood wrestling against each other in a time-contest. A large slab and a tiny slab seem a mortuary representation of motherhood. A chapel buried under ivy—all of it but the rusted iron door.

Different birds attracted to so free an aviary add to the confusion by a variety of tangled nests. An underground natural catacomb, intersected bones that have long since broken through rotten coffins and cemented cells to intermix freely. In this dormitory white coral phalanxes meet: a corpse-to-corpse intermingling of ribs within ribs, more complete than the interpenetration of the human *corps à corps!* Complicity of adulterous earth, wood, leaf, flesh, bone and stone, and all the blended forms of corruption and dissolution of nature, body and mind.

After the hour when the grass is made greenest by the fallen daylight, and a high tangle of grey thistles blurs with the dusk, lovers struggle over the low wall into the ditch, where a pillow of stone awaits their heads and poison-ivy and nettles their hands and knees.

A crown of sharp holly over the head of a still upright grave-stone for those who prefer to stand. Two lover trees joined together within an iron railing unite in vernal post-mortem matrimony.

I, the most faithful of dead shadows, have hovered about this spot since my master-mistress' burial. This is our tomb-stone with an engraved urn—the double of the urn in which their ashes are mingled and sealed together. The love-sick couples that come here prefer this stone bed even to the ditch, unless they be too shy, superstitious or hasty. I throw my darkness over them where-ever they lie. Their warmth makes of me a living shadow. With too much feeding on the night I have grown so thick a covering that I can almost hide them.

A disturbance of light crosses us from the head-lights of a motor, then all falls back into a simplified tangle of starred blossoming branches.

Something unusual is astir in this timeless place. A single foot-fall—an eavesdropper? We are never visited by thieves; they prefer the belated race-winner. Even at daybreak a crime would hardly be detected out there amongst so much dirty scattered paper left after the races. What causes that swirl and sinking of wings? One of the carved angels released from its petrified time-service?

A shot. A suicide amongst the dead? Someone tired of death? A form has risen, or rather a shaped light.

Two other lights cross swords or wings. A struggle of some kind ensues. A grating of moon-blades, a high cry of pain. A sinking of the shaped light. I approach . . . I feel in the air a heaviness of lost wings.

My darkness tries to understand, to complete its sense of the situation.

Many of Death's cast-offs approach the radiation to be incorporated, like separated atoms in a ray of light. Each pleads to be taken into service even as I.

Death is so parsimonious, so little an overweight of baggage is allowed after the sloughing of the flesh that even the "double" and the shadow, though faithful as domestic animals, must hover about, above-board, be left behind, waiting to be born again into the receptive life of some stranger.

"Mon semblable, mon frere," do you take on this unfinished work of woe, and patch out our broken lives?

I was aware of many of the fragments of a once concrete entity. Graveyards are places of infection; not all is taken away by the dead—the diseases of their brain, their last thoughts, their desires, their failures, lurk in the air like poisoned wine to intoxicate the new-comer with the besetting characteristics of the deceased. So much is carried on in this way that those are right who feel that almost nothing of their dead is left in the graves—only the skeleton and its grin. "He laughs best who laughs last."

These, Death's discards, crowd on the living as beggars.

All those who are out of the body must find again a body.

Not to belong to a human make-up, not to become incorporated, not to lead or be led by a shape, is the worst thing that can befall even a shadow. Many dis-embodied fragments that hoped to expand by them-selves nourished false claims, which could not nourish them long. These belated over-proud ones, who would rather perish alone in their diminished littleness than join forces with a composed and organised being, were not amongst the very best survivals; but even some of those, to whom no one had given a form, were drawn into the ever more bent and vibrant light—absorbed into this very inclusive being who seemed to defy sin-gle existence with a never-to-be conciliated choice of opposites.

As earthly rulers have many attendants, counsellors, ministers, minstrels, traitors, so this light, although in-cluding so many personages only remotely connected with its centre, must yet be responsible for them. Keep up a consistent mortal appearance, yet disown none.

I was one of the aspirants the light recoiled from. A revolt seemed to occur each time I drew near to take shape from my new master.

I offered exceptional terms: Unlike the rest I could be almost constantly on service, and take only an hour's rest at high noon, and from midnights without moon replenish my thinness. I promised to muster such darkness into me that I could make light invisible. I would also, of course, disappear upon command, or stand at a distance, or rush ahead, or lag behind, and do all shadowy things that might be expected of me. Was there ever a more willing and responsive Darkness? Had I not already shadowed a master-mistress, a couple so united that I never could cut out one from the other in separate silhouettes.

Still the form of light hesitated, and I divined from this hesitation the angelic origin of our host. To be preceded or followed by a shape of Darkness was the most difficult of concessions for one of these children of Light who live at lowest in mid-ether by means of vibrations and oppositions of radiance. Only when they descend to earth can our laws of darkness beset them.

My varying blot was finally admitted: the Light rose and stood at full height. I rose overshadowing. We started moving in unison, close to each other we glided, without stumbling, as human beings would have stumbled, upon a body lying in the silver grass with dead open eyes. The sound of shot had dispersed the spirits that were still gathered about their lost leader. The wound had made a mouth in the forehead—to give escape to some obsession?

This fallen rider whom a nightmare had thrown seemed neither a man nor a woman. Simultaneously we bent down, a hand of light and a hand of dark opened the cape, touched the thin linen shirt, the stilled chords of the throat, the stopped heart. All lay complexly still as interrupted music—the instrument might serve again?

A substitution suggested itself. The light reflected the dead features as it leant over them—the proud pinched nose, the over-sensitive mouth, the expressionless eyes. The skin still warmed by the blood that stained the short light hair seemed to plead; but my master hesitated before taking on this physical form. Not the same hesitation as in admitting me into its inner circle for its shadow, but more as one would try to refuse too absorbing and burdensome a gift.

CHAPTER II

BROUGHT TO LIFE

THE transfusion of the light into the blood set the physical mechanism going. The great arteries, the veins, began looping their rounds, taking on their complex work, sending a trepidation through the whole frame, turning out from the central motor, sparks, thrills, antennæ of touch, all the productions of consciousness. The glow, the blush, the hesitant vibration, the regular beat. Brought back to life, the human divinity of the senses profoundly sensed. Awake to the feel of the grass-blades against the cheek—each grass-blade encountering a point of sensation.

The hands still turned up to the stars for inscription within their palms, then downward in their grasp on the earth—the feet opening like fans made rhythmic by the palpable breezes.

The body baring itself for communion, receptive of efflux and influx, ready for exchange, taking from passing things their pleasure-hints, unions innocent of possession. Not yet the hunter with nets, the possessor that kills.

Blond body stretching its continent before us, where are the elements that can move and undo its well-adjusted functioning, its tides and seasons?

Great dormant animal completed, but oblivious of care and pain. Safer than the Rose-Garden, this Garden of the Dead. Indolent beast yet to be fed on the sun and the sea, and the flesh that is like and unlike.

All terrestrial beings are solitary, but they would approach to spoil one another's solitudes. Swoon back upon yourself in completed oneness. Be you a paradise unto yourself without serpent or Adam, or a coupling of the beasts, ignorant of the joys that set us sobbing.

Great body, medium by which to realise and partake of this singular life. Extinguish its red torch? More vain than my moving shadow upon you in the air-tide is the first move towards you of hollow resonant steps.

A panic amongst the shadows. A woman between two men advancing within the glade, followed by the guardian's wife with flickering candle, the almond of gold flame with its tiny blue kernel insufficiently shaded by the old parchment hand disperses our moon-feast.

I made for the nearest tangle, a refuge of shrubbery. Missing the entrance, I dilated in fright over the top and fell on a summer-house of ivy: at bay, free to watch the candle retreat and the moonlight spread out again to assemble disbanded shadows grouping themselves about the new-comers.

The woman glowed as though she contained a *chapelle ardente*; the men seemed to have no interior radiance of their own but rather to borrow it from the woman. They walked on either side of her. The one to her right had no full face to speak of, but rather two slices of profile joined together by a crooked smile that had slid in joining, giving an asymmetric aspect to a duplicate of identical features. The higher of the eyes was also distinguished by a piece of round glass.

So fixed a face turned everything into a medal about itself: the moon-mixed background fused and metalled together for this effigy. Even the woman's beauty served to cut out these sharp differences in relief against her own glowing face to which the man on the left bore a resemblance, a worn-out replica, a degenerate issue of the same dynasty. Her lover? Her brother? Her husband? He was subordinate to her as though he were one of her gestures made man. He carried a picnic basket towards a chosen spot in the glade, where a clean sharp stone would do for a table. Their three profiles, suddenly separated by the woman falling out from between them, stopped by the body of my master lying full length at her feet. She bent down to find out whether the pulses had stopped. The monocled profile looking for material traces, picked up the whip, the spurs, the revolver. An upward cut of the mouth expressed a mean smile.

The woman knelt; her hands seemed to sculpture with magnetic heat a yielding shape of clay. She breathed into the pinched nostrils that expanded to her breath. Given over to single elated creation, she hardly heard the profile ask of her:

"What right have you to bring this being back into life? What have you still to offer that is worth this determined peace? Brought back to life, the dead must begin dying all over again, propped up between us as a drunkard and helped home, over the low wall, into the motor. It is now for you to mother this resurrection of yours, held tenderly in your untender arms, the chill of death dispelled by the blaze of your flesh."

The Profile, as a Chorus, commented on the inevitable events before it. A hand released the mechanical horse-power; the four discs of speed carried us on so quickly that we almost outstripped a pursuing scent of lilac from the mob-torn lilac bushes around the bend of the race-course.

I was near enough to my master to realise the surprise experienced at our merely flying along a level. Twice the inquisitive head rose above the car, was shadowed upon the ground, trailed along, mixed up with the wheels. This hugged-road manner of soaring in an embrace left no yearning for the long winged flight of the One. As a magnified pair of night-moths crossed the head-lights my master sighed and settled back more completely into the arms of the woman.

A crackling sound from the road made The Boy with the Basket look down in inquiry. Next to him the high Profile with the eye under glass exclaimed: "Tar and pebbles."

"No, fallen acacia flowers," the woman corrected. "Their scent cries up to us as we pass over them."

And indeed her voice could have made acacias out of pebbles, but it had no need to, for a white shower blew from a tree overhead into her lap. We proceeded more slowly through strata of descending and ascending scent. The crushed acacias smelt the more sweetly, the wheels tossing them upwards as in the tread of a mill. The scent was so cloying that we seemed to taste it.

Close to the near face, the woman's voice continued: "I have borne you into the month of falling acacias and shooting stars. These fireworks, that particular Capricorn design, is always just above me when I love. You remember?"

This avowal of so repetitive an emotion made the One shrink.

She added: "In love you are more than human."

Before a long courtyard ended by a dimly lit house the car stopped. The Profile explained:

"We apologise for this unwelcome restitution. Here is your estate, I return to you your papers, your revolver, your key, your solitude, your home."

"May I add this basket," interrupted the Boy, "for you may be hungry on your return from so disturbed an expedition."

The Profile insisted, tactlessly cutting out his remarks on the sharp features.

"You are not as well off as you were. The night you chose for yourself promised to be more secure. But good-night to you, good-night!" The man and the boy turned away.

The woman's hands seemed again to mould the irresolute shoulders about to depart, to infuse courage, mark her possession, cling as one possessed. She leant as heavily as though she had fallen; when her deep mouth met the lips to which she had again given life, the wound in the forehead throbbed with a reminiscent yet obscure pain.

CHAPTER III

THE OTHER'S HOUSE

AS the car, burrowing its head-lights through a tunnel of night, was becoming invisible, the look between the woman and my master, keyed to so high a tension in the dividing space, finally snapped and recoiled into separation.

No longer held, we made our way towards the house. Our double silhouette—a standing and a prostrate shadow—sounded a single tread on the paved court.

Something uneven underfoot made us bend down. The hand of dark and the hand of light picked up but a fan, a pleated shade, which, when opened, fanned a city perfume into lilac and acacia-haunted nostrils.

The key found the front-door lock with magnetic precision. We entered, rousing the somnolent, housed air. Nobody appeared. We went up-stairs, guided by a light through an open door, into a high mirrored room.

Where are we?

The opposite mirrors through a procession of repeated lights answered: "Here! "The high vaulted ceiling echoed: "Here!"

Adaptable almost to the exclusion of ourselves, limited and shaped according to so suggestive and pre-existing an environment, we gave in to the mood of the things about us.

Dead fires had left many ashes upon the hearth, the candles had almost all burnt down below their quicks, and spluttered wax tears over the pillow of a bed large as a snowdrift—a large empty bed covered with white furs. The white walls bore a bluish sheen of curtains up to the round ceiling, where storm-blue clouds had frescoed their dampness into chance designs more alluring than the precise art-fixed medallions over the doors—two winged griffins pawing a high urn of fruit; Mother-Venus teaching the boy Cupid to shoot and to fly. A barometer hung on the wall, its hand resting at "variable." A closed black piano held in its polished surface slippery midnight reflections, all blended and blurred like music by the soft pedal.

A numbness fell upon us as we approached and lay down on the bed. The down of the pillows had stifled the swan-song of what dreamers? . . . was the question on awaking

"Who are we?" was the question on awaking out of a first sleep.

But questions and answers pursue each other, bend in the same direction but never meet.

The sheets, instead of the crushed silver grasses, made the body miss the ripple of air about the ribs.

A series of remembrances had already taken hold of the senses; the heavy imprint of the woman's body blended with the beat of the blood.

Blood? Have we become a thing of blood?

The One stood up on the bed, confronting the mirror. A simultaneous succession of reflections, more rapid than vibration, gave back through endless corridors of crystal, a body, still partially clothed, the seraphic head charged with new life. The electrical eyes seemed fed from a near battery—that close mesh of blue veins coursing through the temples?

The One looked with wonderment at the mouth-shaped wound of rusty blood, then bathed the stain almost away.

The mirrors recorded the gesture through arcades of watery distance and vistas of drowning lights.

The opened basket, from which a few acacia flowers had fallen, gave forth a sharper odour of food. Even the perfumed fan was laid aside for plovers' eggs, chicken-wings, whole tomatoes with seeds pouring out through their splits in a gurgle of ripeness.

A cardboard platter offered cherries, hard as virgin kisses; apricots, soft as mature cheeks.

While the One ate of mortal food, a cloudiness settled down upon the spirit, that as yet refused the spirits of wine; for a keener drunkenness still shot, at moments, through the confused brain.

We've met with too many persons and allowed them all to cross and join in us. We shall never get ourselves clear now. This collective organism must at least be made harmonious. Let us learn to lead our orchestra, harmonise this variety of selves as composite as a nation that hardly dares shout: "The king is dead, long live the king!"

"Are we no longer a double being? What is this world of separate sensation, of oneness? Who was that woman—so apart? Did she come so near just to leave us more alone?"

"Perhaps she doesn't know to whom she belongs any more than we do! Are all meetings in the flesh as deceptive?"

"What has been our life? The clue—will no one give us the clue?"

"Here we seem to be in a place of half-measures in which to confuse our divine entity, become nebulous as a satellite, a spiritual parvenu, subject to lost currents. To what end?"

"Do we no longer contain our affirmations? Must we ask of outward objects their secrets? Open all those closed doors to interrogate doors, apparently the same on both sides? Have they a wrong and a right side? To be shut in or shut out seems too much alike. Shall we stay here or go elsewhere?"

"By progressing we risk a fall into the past. What past? Yet even the past to which we now somewhat belong must be made to reveal itself. Otherwise how can we act?"

"Supposing some one cried out: 'Who goes there?' What should we be able to answer?"

"Yet we must take courage and examine this house. So vague an inheritance has its responsibilities. We must not appear not to know. Let us ask assistance from passages, from rooms an explanation. Even the memories they contain must become ours."

"Is this aquarium of stagnant air a hall? A veranda? A conservatory?"

Akin to the bare-footed sleep-walker, to the child haunted by wander-lust, we had strayed down to the lower storey.

We balanced ourselves on the glaze of floors on a level with the outside. Those trees with their feet caught in the ground, are they the garden's sentinels?

The guilt-sense of the innocent was upon us. As we opened an outer door on the dead of night, the magic of nocturnal caravans slowly moved through our insomnia—the line with the desert sound in it:

"The camels are coming to town, ha, ha!
The camels are coming to town."

With the first touch of real air we came upon a little temple—for what else could be that Greek-shaped retreat wedged between walls, still holding its own against the background of a distant factory's gigantic chimney, threatening as the Babylonian tower of human sacrifice, its breath flaming above this well-ordained sanctuary built on the brink of revolutions, yet throwing out a little light leading into a higher consciousness of love.

Were those three large candles lit for the dead? The temple—or was it not rather a "Folly"?—had nothing mortuary about it; the stone steps, the four columns of the platform, suggested rather the retreat of some wandering god.

In the interior of the only room, or chapel, no windows, no outlook, once we had closed the sculptured double doors. The three church candles, false symbols of one no longer dead, must be blown out.

27

Here was to be found the beginning of a clue. This is where we had left off. About to put out the first of the three buds of flame, the breath-scattered light pointed lengthwise, illuminating the vellum cover of a large book. A will? Memoirs?

Led by indiscretion and anticipation, we read:

THE LOVE-LIVES OF A.D.

There was an uncanniness in coming so abruptly upon this revelation, not unlike the leavings of a feast in an abandoned oasis, or the frozen crew of some Arctic expedition. Here were to be found traces of the human adventure undergone by our predecessor,—hardly a satisfactory documentation, no names, no dates, no anecdotes. It was for us to gather intuitively what happiness A.D. had been spared, and what sorrows had been undergone, and not count on much material aid from without. Though many phrases were as good as charts to a seafarer, here again we were at sea.

Then again we were on the scent of some inner sensation—some personally captured truth. We engaged in exciting pursuit.

What had been the love stories?

Were these indications as authentic, as satisfactory as the simple narration of an experience?

The quintessence—the extracts—made one long for the single flower, the human touch, a relapse into physical descriptions, something one could grasp, hold, wilt, recognise again in oneself.

A sensation of losing touch made one look for some usual trait, though it might have proved as unenlightening and absurd as the consular registry of "medium mouth, nose, eyes, chin," on a passport. What matter the traveller's appearance? For here was delivered up the inner resemblance. What matter what had been said or done, the course of events, the meetings, the climax, the solution, the outer web of circumstances? Any other tale of events might have served as well. The soul's biography, intact, though fragmentary, had been caught and left to us.

A.D. made us realise that the love-stories we live are hardly ever our own, that their significance dwells in what they lead us to express, or awaken within ourselves. Experience is a loan by which we are revealed. In this spirit we settled down to read.

Nothing formidable, nothing conspicuous, nothing that at first arrested the entire attention, which had to enter a state of subjectivity, as unpretentious as the little temple itself. An aroma of the mind lingering in the mind—the spark of an epigram caught from the troubled love-quests of a fire-fly. Should we not return to so sincere a confessional? The contents of this book might nourish and guide us—we might even learn some parts of it by heart and, when at a loss, recite it as a lesson or a prayer.

It comprised hymns, quotations; poems threw out their antennæ for individual comprehension.

We read our way through an anguish distinct as a cry. Another paragraph so suited our present state that we continued the reading of it within ourselves.

In search of oppositions and differences between A.D. and ourselves, we observed the book, the binding which had pleased our touch. What once living parchment had been stretched into service? Our eyes examined the grain, discovered that the smoothness of either side-cover, when bent back to leave a hollow between them, had once been a human breast.

A repulsion, a hatred seized us. Here was indeed the human touch, the hint at a tragedy of individual flesh. Through the horror of our reactions we missed what this being had suffered.

Misunderstanding the deep significance of so apparent a desecration, ignorant that no cruelties are more keen than those which proceed from an outraged sensitiveness, we suffocated with irrepressible soul-anguish akin to physical sickness. Asphyxiated by the fumes that rose from so condensed a life, the working of so complex a hurt, we knelt, and holding the book to our own breast, vowed allegiance to it. We would revenge the suicide make good the failure, go back in A.D.'s stead, justify the signature, take over this broken destiny, be stronger than life.

Chapter IV

PARTICIPATION

OUTDOORS, in the centre of silence, moonlight silvered into dawn, the irregular beat of the factory started the city's diseased mechanical heart—generous pulsation from out our finger-tips, seemed to circulate through all creation!

An effort beyond self to join with yet uncaptured forces.

No longer separate but mingled with a variety of being, surpassing self for the greater gain: to be all. The ebb of life within charged with life from without.

The whinny of a horse in the uncertain light. A nightmare, or the stable-call of a horse? A staggering towards or away from reality?

In the hall the empty standing boots; or was the invisible owner there? A dawn-shape rising from them?

Again from without, the whinnying of a grey mare in the dawn. A mane in the mist, just over the gate. . . . Action, a spring into the saddle. Away, on that Other's round.

Astride the quivering bones upon the habitual ride.

Wading through alleys of sand freshly combed for the oncoming hoofs, to a high arch cut in the colourless stone of day. Arc de Triomphe—Triumph's dead finish.

The Champs-Elysées, stretching their shaving strop curve, free of the glint of speed sharpening its razor down and up, up and down, to the little Concorde ordered like a mantelpiece, with miniature fountains, the great stone lady-pavement weights holding down the farther end.

The street's blocked floors, roofless apartments, polished by traffic.

The caged Tuileries: a prison for the ghosts of queens and kings.

The green-canvas wagons of the Merovingian *maraîchers*, evenly piled with cabbages, turnips, carrots, cauliflower, lettuces, slowly moving towards the Halles, their drivers asleep on these thrones of vegetable abundance.

Carefully, across a bridge, over the slippery river and dark wet macadam, our way chosen by the horse, our shadow an out-rider hesitating on the house-walls of narrowing streets, and on, past many blind windows and closed doors.

The ash-bins brimming with yesterday's lilacs. The dawn-mare stopped before one of these, nibbling the yet fresh leaves.

A lap-full of acacias before this very door!

Dismount here?

A lump of busy rags was emptying the ash-bins at the end of the little street, among a scurry of disturbed cats.

The ragman approached the opened door, and placed the emptied bin inside.

Tying the bridle to the great door's handle, we stepped in with our shadow. . . .

At the end of an open passage, an arched court. In its midst a basin of cement held a plot of grey grass.

A last bat veered on its last round, its little capes above our head. In a moment the dikes of silence would give in before a flood of sounds. Carrying on the work of the day, servants would be about, and morning equal on all sides.

Windows still shuttered, all but the large one of a studio on the ground floor, its single sheet of glass beginning just above our reach. Our soft boots to the long sill raised us in sight of the interior. A belated greyness hung about several shrouds over dampened covered clay, and heads turned into stone stared white-ly on. Through the watery surface of glass a woman lying asleep.

Our shadow's fall on her, or a clink of spurs, or her action in a dream made her turn. Her eyes were closed, but our shadow between her awakened breasts made her body seem to stare at us. What had those rounded lids of heavy flesh, their triumphant and unmutilated youthfulness, to do with the *peau de chagrin* of that book of torture? To be continued through us? Or simply not to meet the story? To be alive, and refuse a single track of life?

A pairing off with another?

A couple where each renounces innumerable selves?

Had none of those sculptured watchers brought to maturity that body as yet becalmed in careful loves that leave no mark? No evil space between the perfectly joined thighs which seemed to defy parting.

With a dismay of noise, break through her cry and that glass, drowning to reach the inner depths of her?

Not to love seems no easy matter. Only a sheet of glass between, blurred by our breath; return of the breath she gave us.

The warmth of her in our blood. Love-feast on the fallen bedclothes. To leave her under cover of polished water, spell-bound without shift, shutting us out: transparency and insight now but a reflection of ourselves. Yet time to fly? A horse, a horse!

Again past the little closed houses, their stale bourgeois couplings paralysed in sleep. To regain centaurian magnificence, lead and be led by a horse. To breakfast on etherised shreds of air still free of things astir. The sky-changes yet slight, though preparing dawn's colouring chemicals. In pastures dew-fresh to chew the old cud? Or swifter than memory to ride?

A bridal-path: Cours la Reine.

To guard from broadening daylight this over-sensed horse in its sheath of tremulous silk, its foaming flanks not to be seen by machine drivers.

Their horse-power of regulated pistons.

The whole city won over to a race with mechanical life. On its routine the first trolley tight-roping its manufacturing its guiding star. A splutter of crushed diamonds under its wheels as it runs parallel with our sparked hooves and heart-propelled flight!

Behind us the city its toys: its giant hoop, the iron-fretted tower of petty height.

A sailor, with a heavy male-saturated girl in one arm, lurched up from some subterranean passage—the Trocadéro? Its aquarium? Its Métro? His lurching walk evoking Dog-gin and the liquid competition of waves. Down along the river a boy from a canal boat rode a rope-raw limping mule. Did he not feel the raw spot and the limp? It hurts. It hurts us, that old woman's sore eyes. That man carrying too heavy a load is weighing on our shoulders! Is not existence a capacity for becoming all that one senses? Was not this the Cross of Epicurism? Senses cultivated for enjoyment can hardly escape martyrdom.

A whiff of fresh bread from an underground bakery, the street-sweepers with their switch faggots waking the dust—others doing the "*ménage*" of the "châlet de nécessité," and the Punch and Judy show.

Success lies in repetition, not in creation of new outlooks. Everywhere repetition is kept alive in someone's stead.

A down-town drift of people in stupidly complicated clothing was now filling up the vacant places. The workman of leisure with loose wine-coloured corduroy trousers, cagy shirt and comfortably looking on, reading the crowd if it were his illustrated morning paper.

Like a headline, a white young man came too close, striking as a blow.

As we proceeded, each thing as seen from another angle delivered up to us a surprise. The landmarks all displaced made our home-faring another voyage of discovery. Nothing keeps less in its place than the past, a shifting quicksand not to be held by any footprint.

After the living moment, if we should turn back, would we not see the burning city? the pillar of salt? Or just the eyes of the Gorgon turning all into stone?

A glance over our shoulder: safe with our groom of shade on a grotesque mount behind.

No shadow is a hero to its master.

The only other horses about were pulling a hearse to a bastion-like stronghold whose stone prow bore down upon Paris full of its cargo of corpses berthed in mortuary chapels—marble dog-kennels and petrified birthday-cakes of the well-to-do dead. The pall-bearers followed bareheaded. Caught in collective emotion, everyone took off his hat. As the coachman urged the black team uphill, our inner sight X-rayed through the coffin the ceremonious clothes, the bruised decomposition of the flesh, to the architectural sexless skeleton.

We escaped from one graveyard; let us not dwell either here or there.

On the backward ride simultaneous thoughts caught up and came to meet us, incidents recently brought by us into existence rose before us demanding identification and currency. Impressions minted in the mind and evolved, coined in words, stamped into effigies, a chain of sensibility uniting them:

> Again on the sill of her casement?
> Beauty a lure, a trap, a sterility.
> That white-faced morgue-man still to be drowned. . . .

Suicide a love-declaration to life.

That Napoleon-hatted coachman of the hearse. . . .

Better to be king of cabbages; vegetables smell less than corpses?

Cats' tails; lightning-rods.

Phosphorescent eyes charged with a coming storm.

Hoofs and the half-moon. . . .

A wish? A limitation.

Experience a record of wrong choices.

What of the unlived side? The unchosen course.

Go both ways: choose all.

A depopulation in self—a falling-off of our retainers?

Machines have temperaments: accidents.

We, Lady Godiva-ing it, amongst them.

Peeping Tom astir.

Better have our virility in the brain.

Double sex not together. Wasteful.

Angels are hermaphrodites, self-sufficient. No marrying in heaven.

On earth they often appear with a woman's body and a man's desire, or vice versa.

Two needed—No one entirely a woman or a man?

Infinite variety of couples and couplings.

That sailor and his girl looked inseparable—

On long cruises, double nature given a chance.

A need with men. And what for women?

That woman. The eyes of her body still upon us, her warmth clinging to our blood.

Her imprint, a lack in us. The hunger of our want?

Maternal love. There is also maternal hate.

Who are we? A collective emotion.

No chance of being alone.

Even the beat of the gallop echoed rhythms from the haunting book. Accompanying our pace with fragments of poems broken up like kindling wood to serve a new fire.

Is this dancing light a being by day?

I no longer see, hear, feel or breathe according to your laws.

Nor love you, Psyche, half-caught in the flesh.

Yet I would thank you that you did not detain me,

Nor feed me, nor drug me to sleep in your body.

Nor bury me in living.

Your servitudes have freed me.

Disunited and seeking completion.

Without you I am that other self

That has been denied burial in you,—

That One to Oneness returning.

For a breathing space we had joined the uncreated present.

A shower broke from the rising sun. A wind-blown flying shower, a rage of rain, shattered mirrors about us. Seeking shelter, we entered the gates and dismounted in sight of the stables. The retreating dappled grey back seemed nothing more real than the painted wooden horse of a merry-go-round. Lost, the chance of child-hood and a gold ring? The spirit of adventure become a habit? Through a field of high grasses a scythe has ceased from mooning its half-moon way. Though the rain had quieted, a cataract was still pouring over the broad eaves.

Under the curdling white shirt the One appeared drenched to nakedness. The rhododendrons' reflection made a stained-glass of the transparent flushed cheeks and the translucid eyes. The thin enamel of the teeth let the under-light through. Broken prisms were playing about everywhere. The base of a rainbow feeding with fresh colours the pigment of the flowers. The One ran out to join the farther end, finding its span too far for soggy boots, stopped by a low wall. Four wires were stretched over the broken part of the wall to prevent too easy an access. The raindrops clinging to these silver limes seemed a crystalline annotation of music. Was not this the very same place transformed by day? The matted trees and underbrush had added to their tangled meshes a jewel-work of scintillating raindrops, which in falling had refreshed the old tombs. Washed white by the rain or quite new, a hitherto unnoticed slab bore this epitaph—"Time has made, to mock at my heart, a tombstone," and *S. de la C.D.*

The One continued reading with closed eyes: the epitaph on the tomb and the epigraph in the book were the same. A panic ran through the arteries—a terror seeking refuge in the cells of the heart. A foreboding shook the kneeling form, or was it simply a shiver from the penetrating cold of wet clothes? How rid ourselves of this life of deadly repetition, reintegrate the incarnate state? The prisoned ribs rose with sighing like wings.

Shaking off a cluster of rain-notes from the vibrating wires, the One vaulted over the wall and ran around the bend of the race-track. I, the shadow, winning the race past the lilac bushes, the acacia trees, their sweets sickening in the morning air.

As on the previous night, nobody appeared on the threshold, no sound disturbed the darkened room. Softly dividing the united sheen, the high window curtains were pulled apart.

In calcium daylight could the uncertain forces appear?

Had exercise made our health normal to the exclusion of self, to a disbanding of our legion?

Which were we?

Were we after all but a survival, more and more at home in another's house?

A return to pillows saturated with dead breath?

The bed had been made during our absence. A golden Chinese wrapper of cool silk and protective dragons lay upon it. A well-tended house of invisible servants.

No paradise without an overseer.

Our arms went out in anticipation. In so short a time had freedom become solitude and solitude loneliness?

As we threw off the wet clothes, the distinct mirrors gave us our shining double . . . revealed two blade-smooth scars across the chest

The *peau de chagrin* binding had been taken from our own flesh.

CHAPTER V

CORRESPONDENCE

Love, take me back to you and make me whole,
Who am divided and in unbelief,
An infidel in thought and word and grief,
A double heart and a promiscuous soul!

THIS, and many other appeals, insinuated themselves from the book through us, vivifying the outward wounds, the hurts within.

Another's life was hot upon us.

We failed to understand: We saw only what we saw in the sharpened light dealt through the windows.

Some flesh may be predestined to scars, as the best of fruit to a silver knife.

After all, how little any of us knows of the life lived.

Like an orphan, we had been adopted into a family of Events.

Why had we been chosen?

Why were we no longer distinct?

Our legion had obscured our command.

Who would arise from this malaxation of selves?

. . . Exercise a divine right?

Who is to be the leader of these invading and opposed forces?

We were as a lifeboat crowded with too many passengers—overcrowded to sinking! Whom throw out?

Whom should we fall back on? Save?

What wreckage had called us into service?

To fight for what cargo of lost lives?

Had we so soon forgotten our mission to make good the failure—to mend the broken spirit of the body we now tenanted?

Who had not answered the prayer, that we must answer it?

What intercession of despair had we come to arrange?

What desertion had called us into the danger-zone?

This was no dream-drama, but the stigmata of a partial destruction.

Had we not been found as good as dead?

As we cannot well remember, let us move on to forget.

Movement backward or forward?

If we turn to go out, will someone knife us in the back?

Where is our shadow?

Day the disperser, deliver us, cut apart, cut through these thoughts!

Clothed in A.D.'s wrapper, from the *lit de repos* between the wall and table, we touched the fan we had picked up the night before intended for A.D.

We examined the monogram, "S. de la C.D." Again the same!

Who was this wanderer, with scented fan in hand from the yards of the dead?

Or had A.D. inadvertently let it fall on the way there?

Should we open the ivory sticks? Disclose their story?

Lace-covered like mittened skeleton fingers. . . .

On the outer side, the stick bore an ivy-leaf design into which was interlaced: "You had the ivory of my life to carve."

As the blindfolded in a game, lunging through mystifications, grasps at any certitude, we recognised that the fan we held had in some way determined A.D.'s suicide.

The air is heavy with ungranted prayers: "Love take me back to you and make me whole."

And what an answer of reproach: "You had the ivory of my life to carve."

The romantic dependence—the persistent coupling, a sickness of the soul or of the senses?

Which had A.D. tried to overcome?

Or was it an attempt to brand and dry up a surviving sensuality, and so escape from physical laws that in some way were found limiting?

A growing state of discovery seemed to lead us.

An inheritance? Subjective intuition?

Or were we merely seized from outside—up against "hard facts" like a dog hind-legging cement?

Were we caught as a fish? or so full, so pregnant, so grafted with another that we must lose ourselves?

Were we already so given over as to no longer be the centre of our own volition?

Had we reached so near the border-line that the slightest urge might deflect us—topple us over, leave us to the mercy of any madness?

If we were not to regain our supremacy and concentration, our diamond hardness free of the diamond's dark life of crystallisation—might we not at least keep a balance?

Pendulate between excesses until the hour strike!

Our chorus continued:—

We can judge of nothing while we are in it.

Even happiness is an aftermath.

Only the retired dealers in reality can realise.

To touch with the senses is so limited that even Epicurus' enjoyment became abstract that he might taste of it. . . .

The "mind's-eye" is the vitalising factor of sensations, wherein sensations are chosen to become sentiments—to lead us on.

A choice—a lead from the unconscious. Its dictates at loose ends.

Let us go a-gathering!

Reserve essentials.

Nor be attacked and overpowered by hangers-on in the by-ways of self!

A panel in the wall revolved.

A breakfast tray on the dumb-waiter announced breakfast.

Hot water, a crystal pot of tea. The tea smelt of the jasmine flowers that floated on the surface separate from the submerged tea-leaves.

Tea at best is a scent we may drink.

Toast-eating—a rumbling over cobble-stones.

Rather bite into a soothing apricot leaving an imprint of our teeth, as we finger A.D.'s neglected letters.

In this dead-letter office, to open, to unfold pages hardly meant for us.

To way-lay these dove-carriers of inscriptions, their arabesques conducting to intimate places of the heart—labyrinthine paths of writing, misleading us to what bowers?

Their secrets ours or not ours?

Have we not all opened letters seemingly not addressed to us, yet somehow intended for us? developing under our eyes some circumstances belonging to us, that it would otherwise have taken us long to unravel.

Indiscretions are short cuts!

We wore another's wounds, hadn't we a right to a correspondence that might account for them?

Now that we were the representative of A.D.'s house, the loves and letters came to us by a natural sequence, a right of succession.

None of the errors of legality that direct things to a wrong heir.

We recognised so apparent a claim, warranted by our presence in another's body, which would little by little render us master of the situation: our heritage, all A.D. had suffered and possessed.

Our more than entire entity took in pity these life-divided ones—would see what post-mortem reconciliation could be effected.

As eavesdropping on another self, we cautiously parted an envelope.

A leaning handwriting like a coursing greyhound ran across the pages, and seemed to bear in no wise on the subject under cover.

MON SEIGNEUR, MA DAME,
You do not consider my orations of silence . . . I who love you infinitely.

Many such superlatives rushed past with just as little stress or meaning in them—superlatives without creation. The unborn passion of a novice being able to realise nothing here, investing all her hope in hereafter. A.D.'s double being had evidently found it easy to feed so nebulous a want, a case so self-engrossed that nothing outside itself mattered to it: "My love for you, which is none of your affair!"

Then again, harping on the untuned string: "I who love you infinitely." To love infinitely may be to love infinitely little!

Immature, morbid, virginal love: green rottenness!

As self-centred, as obtuse as this dealer in infinitudes, the next confession was in a full writing that entwined us, came near as a breath: "While I overrated you what pleasure you might have given me." This well-balanced sensualist would use her lover as an instrument—an instrument of precision not easily to be dispensed with? The words that followed were so precise, so carnal, that we almost felt the heave of her soft ripe belly—contrasting with the tight-skinned maiden, untried yet found wanting, pure as her maiden-letter, from lack of circulation.

Though all are born, few are living: obtuse or oversensed, faulty reflexes, averages, still-birth carried into no vivifying atmosphere, made in series and unmade, deteriorated by use or discovered to be defective.

The choice of such opposites indicated a fatigue in A.D. A fatigue soon to single out and hunt down a diversity of beauty—like any other sense-vulgarian. Descended on a quite physical plane, passions become so located in sexual habits that only in change can they again find the elements that composed their intensity; even the change of passing on into other couples: "Whenever I meet convincing love your name is on my lips."

As there is a constancy carried on in change, so also old couples often rejuvenate their unions: "Give new life to us, we are a changeling pair under your hands."

We seemed to be excluded by a time-limit from the following letter. It sought to alleviate some acute state that, at so late an hour, must have found relief or passed on:

My Stimulant, My Drug!

How cruel to leave me, who cannot disintoxicate myself of you—the laws of attraction impeded for you and not for me who remain in the necessity of you, to draw you ever into me. Why was my flesh not made to capture your flesh? Why do you leave me alone in these pangs that you cause? What has become of the silence around you—you the prodigal in joy. . . .

Next we notice a pink card with an apple-blossom embossed in one corner, laboriously chyprescented. A note without stamp from a neighbouring house? In a servant-like lettering:

The trees have thickened between our two gardens to hide you from your Flore. Will you never receive me even for a moment, my dear little unknown friend? Why are your windows unlit in the evening? You see no one? And what of all your costumes and metamorphoses? Your house, your life is haunted. Have I guessed your secret? Whenever I catch a glimpse of you through my opera-glasses (forgive this approach from which you have no defence!) I see a cobweb of worry spread over your features. I would brush it away with my kisses. Let me come to you. For two years I have lived only by my eyes on you.

Boundless servant-love, given, unasked for—love without quality!
After the near stranger, the distant disciple.

The news, belated, of your catastrophe was hardly felt by me. Yet, the putting on the contact I got a shock through you that I find it hard to stand, and I separate myself again from the disaster of another's pain over which I am worse than powerless. Forgive this lack of depth you have created in me. Since you so adequately fed on my vitals, alias soul, I have become but the outline of my former self, all that these immature States demand. Even in this new world it required a year of self-discipline, this bringing of myself to the surface, this turning of the inside out! I am now attentive to what is about me; I graduate from the present. I live now on frozen game—small game!

We approved A.D. for not having been delayed and lost in these lost women—for breaking whatever might be broken. And what affinity was there to be found in them? It is only by the love we give that we are held. The love we give is the love we want. And how could this specialist in small game, or the love-drugged, or the opulent lady of the second letter, hold in her Venusberg such a one?

Such a one? What did we know of "Such a one? Were we such a one, was such a one of us? These women resembled each other, for nothing fundamental seemed to have determined their choice. The necessity pre-existed in them and A.D. appeared as a developing circumstance rather than as a cause.

The next letter, evidently in a man's hand-writing, struck a deeper note, touched on a theme to which we responded:

> You had her by the heart-strings, but though you are artful and tender, you played neither fairly nor kindly on so great an instrument, and so you have lost her. Though she was one of life's masters she sacrificed everything for you, and it is a just return that you be sacrificed and find no savour left in the things for which you neglected her!—That you are inconsolable alone justifies her death. There is something hard and aloof in you that prevents pity, but rather rouses surprise and envy at so exclusive a despair in one so inhuman. . . .

> Ta cruauté: diamant contre diamant
> Tu travailles à vif dans la matière pure
> D'une étoile . . . ange pris dans ce charnel roman.

What experimentalist, what specialist was this? The writing table appeared to us awful as an operating table—the headquarters of some intelligence office for the affairs of the heart. Wire systems connecting with the campaigns of a multitude of fighters, under fire, wounded, deserted or killed.

There was also a letter to prove that A.D. had sec-onded them in their hour of need, was there to close their eyes—and scrutinize the closing:

> You answer prayers, you tend extremes, a night-guard, a watcher of symptoms by the fever-patient—to take their temperature, to be often wasted on experiments that have not caught fire! They know neither themselves nor the life they are in, but they call to you for help. They make love-signals of distress. You are an answerer of long distance calls; countless wires vibrate messages to which you must respond. Polarised by each, you answer each in turn. You operate them of environ-ment, finally to give them back to themselves.

It was this gift: "back to themselves" that few seemed to appreciate.

Yet A.D.'s mission was a mission of love and of a passing on:

> That you may belong to everything and that everything be yours, inclusive of your-self.

A letter of condolence from a devout friend touched us more than the exposer of A.D.'s erroneous system brought to so full a stop.

> Alas, for our separate hells! How bury gold hair?
> You, who have experienced her death will know how not to believe in it.

As you wrote: "Her death that finishes my life"
will open to you a real world.

Such grief demands supernatural aid.

Call out, you shall be answered.

To be found worthy of so solitary a sorrow is
indeed to take away

> "O grave thy victory,
> O death thy sting."

But senses are persistent. With what horror A.D.
must have enjoyed their survival.

Several letters and a *pneumatique* in the same shaded
back-handed virulent writing tempted the weak-lover
again to a strength found in this weakness:

> What, no more that bright creature insanely
> advancing?
>
> Must I no longer come to you over-keeled by
> transports of giddiness, I mad amongst your sheets,
> your bright body no longer waiting?
>
> . . . In whose boat now do you lie—framboise
> mouth and breasts to the sky . . . ?
>
> It would seem I do not believe in death then. . . . I
> who cannot believe in your grief, in your ashes. You
> have a charmed soul. Because I am jealous I want
> you to prove to me by a sacrilege. . . .

As we were turning the page a voice interrupted us,
broke into the room.

A voice without any body or any breath. Merely
the audible presence. The Glow-woman speaking

dreamily as though from the next pillow, after a night in the same sleep: "Did I wake you? . . . You were in my thoughts before waking . . . . Let us resume. . . . A heat-wave is upon us. Summer never lasts but two or three days. Let us profit. In an hour before your house—just where we left off."

Finding near the bed-curtain the telephone's small cornucopia, we filled it with promises.

It was almost eight by the clock that led its regular life under the barometer stopped at "Variable." The unfinished *pneumatique* and other letters? We would read them later, and gathering their scattered leaves together, we bid them *au revoir*.

Into the next room in search of a change of clothes we found everything prepared for us—even to a warm bath opalescent with bath salts—acacia? Such persistent though invisible an attendance would prove monotonous. We should be glad to leave too well appointed a house, and a romanticism suited neither to the times nor to many of our own natures. So Eros left Psyche—or was it Psyche left Eros? The awkward lamp to blame, or too well regulated a felicity? Nobody can stand unmolested happiness exclusive of most of our faculties. In love, as in other governments, the great unemployed make for revolution. Who would watch over our sleep for our undoing?

Meantime to let us leave the half-secrets of that mail of mistresses! Wonder no more but relax in so well-prepared a bath.

The body of water formed about us. Its loose hermetic embrace warmer than woman? Closer than woman? Comprehending us fully, leaving nothing out of it, but our head—unaccompanied—unkissed.

Our flesh deep, nacreous—the pearls and water-weeds of us now afloat, now immersed in a warmth like our own.

Sunk into the mirror that gives to our shapes, our weight vanishes. Water-winged flatterer, are those diaphanous water-lilies our blood-filled hands? Water-lover, would she never be as simple as water about us?

Then the cooling off, the leave-taking.

The iridescence smooth-gliding, its water-volume diminished, gone from us, dimpling away down the sink!

The memory of it reduced to tears running over our shivering body as we stand in the empty tub.

Chapter VI

A DAY IN THE COUNTRY

B OTH of us early in the meeting met with surprise.
The two on the front seat, prudent as chess-
players, moved slightly in recognition, then settled
back again upon the padding of the car.

The Glow-woman, even more glowing by day, re-
joined looks with us, drawing us back into the same
place next to her.

What game was before us? What rules?

Resembling a well-screened film, not a gesture too
much, not an unnecessary word.

We started on a dust-laid road, then along the River
Seine to the Suresnes *octroi,* where many other motors
were drawn up, their occupants taking advantage of
the heat and holiday.

Women in masks seated by men in beards; some
sphinx-like heads bound up in leather helmets.
Women or men?

Communicating mysteries, most known of each
other at a half-glance?

The morning light accentuated only those traits
by which the Glow-woman and the boy differed. His

55

Longhi mask of a face, we now observed, had no relation to her features which imposed a new proportion, distanced all the other faces. Only a beauty that has the power of renewal is life-enhancing. And so we gazed into her face perfected for our sensation—or was it our sensation perfected by her face? Receptive as molten metal of her beauty only. We did not wish this domination; it came to us out of a clear sky with just this profile upon it.

What had become of the others?

The monocled automaton at the wheel resumed speed. We telescoped roads that seemed to pass into us: motor hieroglyphs shown up in succession more eventful than the incidents they signalled.

The wind banged its tins about our ears.

We gasped, suffocating in too much air that set every loose thing flapping.

Fixed in the flashlight of day, we had become the immovable centres of velocity. We dared not think or assert any part: human packages carried on, to be delivered at some terminus on which our driver alone seemed bent, for he was evidently driving us somewhere. Or was he just an irresponsible figure-head, a superior piece of self-willed machinery? His monocled profile and his sharp naked eye pivoted alternately: starboard, larboard. The hedges were tossed and thrown aside, the trees ran in the opposite direction or narrowed into an ambush before us. The poplars went up like sky-rockets, their striped shadows fell ladder-like in the dust; a black shiny road stretched as the barrel of a rifle along which we aimed and were shot—into the dust again. A brood of chickens, limping on both legs, scurried off on insufficient wings. Once, on the top of a long hill, we slowed down and stopped before the blue-oblong-breasted-red-machine woman who nourished the motor. The heat caught up and settled down in the dust about us.

On the far side we dominated a city of spires and spiritual and commercial masterpieces, bridges: the sculptured flights of a cathedral, stone spires side-by-side with the ironworks of civil engineering.

A suspended bridge under which seafaring ships whistled to one another, while the chimes of many churches advertised the hour. The jumble of bells shaped into distended sound eleven or twelve strokes? Growing spheres of air circling out from each other, haloing the invisible maiden-saint of Rouen, burnt, canonised, staged.

A recent and allied English occupation had staked and left just black-and-white road signs: "Upper Road," "River Road," "Around Rouen."

The Longhi-faced boy was pointing out to the Glow-woman the only ugly building in sight: some barracks in which he "had been detained as a soldier during the first three months of the war before he got exempted."

The monocled profile tried in turn to monopolise her attention by allusions to his military career: "Chauffeur to a superior in rank whose wife was his mistress, which amounted to a balance of powers."

The machine-woman's umbilical tube had been taken from our motor to another. A motorcycle passed us, perforating, ripping in two the heavy summer air by the metre and kilometre. The give of the heat fell back again upon itself as we circled above the town . . . passed stretches of forests, and moving shade-spots on gold, leoparding the forests. A widening sea-smelling river, diamonds riding on the current, or being cut and turned out by the stern of ships opening a peacock tail in their wake.

We reached a market-place where a market was just breaking up, packing into carrioles the leftover vegetables and live-stock.

Our feet touched the ground, subject again to their own volition and self-government. Our appetites swept over the counters.

A three months old kid cleared up the lopped branches and approached us for more, kissing our hand that smelt of the Glow-woman's hand. In greed and erotic confusion he rose full against us, but the short rope brought him down to a four-hoofed fiasco, curtailing our freize of its final development.

Summing up a total, the linen cornets of the utilitarian nuns of Priapus nodded over accounts, flushed by an orgy of calvados and bargaining.

Near by, the sea reached through a double line of cabins; the old-fashioned wooden ones smelling of sand and urine stood behind a row of the new cement and mosaic *cabines de luxe*.

The Glow-woman disappeared into one of these: No. 28—just about her age? The monocled automaton treading the plank on squeaking shoes (Don Juan should move on silent feet) followed into the next cabin.

Male and female partitioned off by separating cells, cemented away from each other—naked in vexing isolation.

Luxury has its drawbacks:
No more looking through the slits.

Left with her boy husband, our cold shoulder of observation turned to him.

His facial series already too well registered: affectation and self-consciousness, affirming some unproved importance within.

Sand-seated near each other in embarrassed intimacy, conversation, in the manner of a dog, between us, waiting anxiously for each to throw the stone.

He seemed only half alive, and never the right half.

Having now to face averted facts, we questioned:

Could this effete epicene be the possessor of the Glow-woman?

When a woman has too much beauty for one, learn how to share her.

We may have muttered the last part of this reflection, for the Longhi-mask answered:

Ecco qui crescera i nostri amori.*

Then, through the bleached face, the help-imploring eyes: "You won't try to escape us again, will you? I much prefer your success to Duthiers'."

---

* Behold one who will increase our love.

59

He pleaded as though his happiness depended upon it. Then he bent down and kissed our nearest sand-embedded hand.

Feeling no response, our eyes, used by one of our worldly inmates, detailed this bathing factory turning out a stripped bourgeoisie of all shapes, sizes, ages, sexes; mature convicts condemned to do their bit of hard labour against the wind and waves, resting on glaring sands, their bodies packed in bathing suits like potatoes in sacks. Varicose legs, bulgy as Christmas stockings, the dead feet of men half buried or afloat:

> Up his nose and his toes
> Dead feet of a man
> As off floating he goes.

Young men, too, but always the feet stamped death-like in the sand. Nothing noticeable about them standardised as they were—only a gorilla variance of hair on the chest, back and legs.

"One man's as good as another." Why are women always trying to forget so consoling a fact?

Fairer to look at a strenuous adolescence, androgynous through exercise, male hardly distinguishable from female. Long legs bared for sunburn; muscles serpenting their way along boyish arms and torso of neat-fitting skin white from winter's indoor gymnasia.

Men have skins but women have flesh—flesh that takes and gives light.

Surely a girl's, that delicately cartilaged shoulder and expectant turn of head?

Hers the cheek where blood and rouge meet in a conflagration of colours. Maidenhood, still half virginally, already cosmetically, blushes.

Ah, but the women, their drooping breasts too small to be falling, their chins not allowed to double below their cropped hair: youth retained, re-engaged in beauty parlours! Petty tortures self-inflicted daily, comparable with the flagellation and hair shirt of monks. These ascetics, ardent to save not their souls but their figures— with which they find so little to do! Big with child, yes, perhaps, sometimes, by accident. There they are, the children, drunk with fresh life, titubating along the beach, big with breakfast, milk-bellies distended against the horizon. The school-broken boys with sailing boats in hand; they dare not put to sea, paying homage in shells to an infant Venus, her straight brows of authority full of their own radiance under hair of curled light, the rest of her quite nude, even to the cleft of her body. "Superfine—what will you do to redeem it?" Middle-aged women to tend her, with thinking faces, women that had let life go past their bodies unused, unsatisfied—still young in places.

Heads and bodies that don't match.

Others with youthful baby faces above their flesh-slides, smiling oblivious over a wreckage of deformities—misused old seafarers, cargoes of spoilt treasures, believing themselves to be the same as at their launching. Women only have such a variety of surprises. At the turning point, choose the face or the figure? Sacrifice the face to the figure, or the figure to the face?

Now and again a creation accidentally perfect—but not allowed long to remain so.

A luxurious and luxuriant womanhood, sleek-helmeted, rounded as shining sea-lions washed up by the last wave.

Youths with enormous hands detaching their camphor-smelling bathing tights plastered to their chests, or drying themselves in the sands and sun near cabins where at 12.45 all drop into formulas and collars. Gone the free arms and legs—the halter awaits each of these fair weather prisoners.

Even their ocean is roped in, marked with danger signals—to tempt good swimmers to the horizon? Some escape by drowning, some by standing apart.

That woman at the opposite end of the beach, fairer than all, demanding neglect as others sought approval—she alone seemed aloof, free. Join her? She needed no joining! Complete unto herself and self-sufficient. Her magical circle inclusive only of herself. A physical intelligence regulated her gestures, making her wonderful to watch, varying ever within herself.

Just arrived an English "fast set": that "Frivolity Girl" in her Callot sea-serpent orange-and-green bathing suit, a limping harlequin in her suits to make laughter for her, and wave-fun, and love.

A salmon fleshed man of the over-matured American Greek type, with muscular breasts, in weight-removing water, buoyant as a danseuse.

A courtesan of the last century bestowing on propagandist breezes a trail of alcove scent, lifting above the breakers statuesque fragments, shaved arm-pits, still shapely wrists encircled with bracelets of crystal, spangled with drops of ocean. Already more than sex-deep in the slippery waves, their foaming onslaught meeting her submerged but firmly buttressed buttocks.

Why is she so long undressing?

Doing her face after the motor trip in the distorted little mirror (the speciality of bathing-cabins and servants' bedrooms)?

A convenience deciding that some are only servants?

Resume the glare?

Unapparent but drastic reasons regulate the functioning of all these people.

How much wiser the social systems of bees and ants.

The matriarchate had its justification.

Men create life too easily not to waste it.

One of our low characters observed that man should wear a more thickly woven *maillot*.

Fathers, with sleek-brushed, sea-sticky hair, buy the daily news before lunching at little tables with their progeniture and female lot gathered about them; through lack of discernment, paralysed in routine— not minding, having chosen, or been chosen, once for all—and once for all, wrong.

The barrack life of that hotel de luxe absorbs them. They will eat of:

Bread without vitamine.
Lobster and mayonnaise tasting of soap.
Eggs of sulphur.
Chicken of its metal cover and dish water.
The salad a sponge of vinegar.
The pastry of elevator oil.
The fruits of unripeness.
The wines opened too late or too soon, with no "bouquet" to the great names on labels.

Late in the mid-day, intellectuals appeared—intellectual even in body, awkwardly advancing their ill-gained importance amongst the chairs all turned like weather-cocks in the same direction. Bruised celebrities, pushing their way on as in perambulators, expecting even the empty chairs to turn round and look at them. Fraudulent usurpers of fame, mind-pickers, culture-snobs.

Like politicians, in favour and out of favour.

Reading the public as brokers read the stock exchange, registering a fall in value at a glance. Readjusting their budget of popularity as well as they may. Paying court with as many *nuances* and modulated bows as the situation demands. Kissing the hand of a silly old *mondaine* with wig of short gilded hair, rounds of giggles and wrinkles and pearls: Desdemona at sixty!

A fatigued innocence in the sunken eye sockets interrupted womanhood that nothing would smother—galvanised in the appearance of youth for ever. One of Voronoff's preservatives.

How to get rid of the faces of those *viveurs*, real, too real, crevassed by the hard light driving its diamonds into their arthritic flesh.

Coty perfume pervading whiffs of sea and the increasing smell of food.

The early lunchers' cigarettes and cigars and coffee outdoors—and the bill, no longer carelessly glanced over, but looked into as a serious attack on income.

A mannishly dressed woman with a fortune, and a mistress in her own right, was managing the difficult table question with the abstract power of her renowned tips, ordering the waiters about as no man would dare.

As the hour advanced, the bald-headed capitalist sought the shade of the international indoor palm-tree.

Couples, carefully not together, went up to their bedrooms.

Sad repetition of conjugal and other loves—far less diverting with its thirty-two positions (who has retained interest enough in the sex-game to try each of them?) than the collective emotion to be obtained from "Shoot the shoots," the "Montagne Russe," "Vers l'Abîme"—exercises in which, after a few little shrieks, one is deposited at the entrance much as before starting.

Now that they were dressed they looked all alike—fashion, a finishing school, turning out neither nobility of skeleton nor maturity of flesh. How would anyone recognize his wife or mistress—adultery, discouraged through sameness, seemed impossible.

The Glow-woman had at last issued on pouter-pigeon feet from her cabin to draw a deep sea breath. Some fresh air still left for her?

No lover rushed from us to meet her.

The high noon light, hard to bear as the detailing stare of a child, found her implacable,—Aphrodite, in form and feature. So did the belated bathers watching her. She was so obviously beautiful and to the general taste that we felt ashamed of sharing in so collective a choice. Her half-husband, he also, gloated over the general admiration, taking it to his loins. Where *he* found stimulus, our sensualist, who had been insepa-rable from the lover, joined our fault-finder.

> She's academic almost to affectation.
>
> Some physical culture still clinging to her.
>
> Her movements made from without, unlyrical, unrhythmic, uninspired. We had expected some new music from her going seaward. There was no music in her feet.

Looking down at the feet of Duthiers that still fol-lowed hers, we burst out laughing, as wave upon wave, breaking into whiteness, seemed to be laughing too at their unaccustomed strangeness.

Other people's toes, even though they seem beau-tiful to their owners, are always a surprise, a shock to behold.

Surely the Glow-woman had never seen Duthiers' feet naked before.
Unused to their ugliness,
Not yet her lover?

So she stood on the glittering sea edge still laughing over Duthiers' feet, the sun playing up and down her keyboard of teeth, and the water breaking into peals of laughter on the shore.

Duthiers dipped in, shivered, and returned to dress.

Going apart alone, she bent down and communed with the holy waters, then high-stepped through churning sea-lace designs, the sea-spin spread white beneath her as her undressing, waylaying her unfeminine knees, her athletic thighs. Now over-striding this changing sea-lingerie to meet the dolphin-backed succession of waves—aswim past their breaking. Her face sun-struck, embedded in the liquid, beyond depth, moving with its motion. Lost in the sea—saved from the land.

Our Laureate apostrophising:

As a wave unfurled upon thee
     Wave upon wave
To rise and break and break and rise together
     and be blended and remoulded
     and remade separate
To toss thee skyward
To throw thee drowned and lifeless upon the sands
     The rolling sea-choir in thine ears
          Filled to the sinking.

For thou art a sea fruit of change and salt
And there is no satiety in the love of sea sisters
And nothing on these dizzy sands is as it seems.

Now saved from the sea—lost in the land, she presently stood before us, freshly salted, dressed, painted in ochre radiance, ready for lunch.

Through habit the three fell into their usual symmetry, leaving the one to go before or pick up their group in the rear.

Break through their fixed pattern?

Cast out a devil to lie at her feet and trip them up?

Get on our sea-legs, or stop the life throb in her throat?

Kick free of all second-rate sentiments? Or love at first sight, that there need be no second?

A dizziness?

Reminiscence?

The glare?

The waves.

Her laugh?

Our hunger?

Focussed back into the present, worthy of a more adequate food, the four of us motored past the simili Palace Hotel.

A stretch of farmhouses, pine, cliffs flushed pink as though they were coming to life.

In France, near every international "Palace" there is to be found an authentic cuisine.

A lane leading to maiden-vine, sun-filtered arbours.

The three entered making their customary triangle.

A pleasure league? A trinity of interests?

What solidarity united them for and against the One?

A shadow fell upon the plate before us making our foretaste ashen.

Our Sensualist, revived by a sniff of the wholesome menu, began lunch on a salad of shrimps with ciboulette, and ended with coffee, and cassis sipped with eyes on her eyes. Then *cartes postales avec tout ce qu'il faut pour écrire.*

Where had we seen her handwriting before? In A.D.'s letters?

One of those letters? Which one?

The interrupted *pneumatique?* Must be verified on returning.

A bee entered our arbour—attracted by the Glow-woman's freshly applied scent, or by the over-ripe raspberries?

Duthiers scooped it away with a sensitive hand that seemed not to belong to his automaton. His fingers were flushed as a nymph's legs, but the bee escaped them and followed air geometrics in buzzing flight, then returned in a bee-line, intent—a spark with resolute sting, which this time Duthiers tried in vain to kill.

We closed a scooped hand loosely about it and took the sting into our right palm.

She smiled on us a new moon.

"Which did you wish to spare?"

To meet such situations with petty acts of courtesy and invention, is part of a lover's art. . . . That such a simple gesture as the spreading of Sir Walter Raleigh's cloak under his queen's feet should have come down to us with that last Cleopatra's miserable pearl-melting flattery, instead of procuring Antony a less acid wine, proves how few attend to this neglected art.

"Women respond too easily to such gestures—the minor poetry of courtship.

"They respond equally well to neglect.

"Women are essentially responsive to everything."

So Duthiers tried to sneer us out of our vantage-ground that the Glow-woman's favour had given us over her habit-drugged adorers.

They could only act repetitively in a given circle in which they had bound themselves and one another. A masked opponent makes a new pass, and they are disarmed.

Duthiers rallied. You have no excuse for not being pliable—on your guard—having just come gives a new back to life rid of your rust . . . gives a new alertness. . . . Suicide a sort of health cure.

"You stand much improved. You've had a change, a change for the better."

Then, on the strength of the champagne, the boy husband continued with an air of appalling complicity:

"We are crystallised in our choice. Deliver us from

the evil of blind habit—we might as well be dead!"

She rises, she awakens from our dead midst.

Follow her mossing height?

He sidled to me, continuing his whispered confession:

"The Glow-woman and I are fixed beyond our reach, nothing gets hold of us. You see her fresh sparkling eyes. I am so drugged that, without you, I no longer see her at all.

"You know our situation. We expect you to renew us—make us over, we no longer feel our love for each other; wake us up to our good fortune. If you don't, *he* will. She's on the war-path, and you're only half an enemy. You interest her more than ever; you have done things she does not expect, you've responded to a live angle of her star."

He again kissed my hand—the stung one.

"You have won the day. Farewell, we must go back."

Duthiers took his seat at the wheel. The boy-husband handed us a small parcel:

"In case you ever get hungry again.

"Remember the last train is at 00.3."

The Glow-woman's voice emphasised their retreat:

"I shall be there."

They were off on backward roads in the smooth gliding car, so fool-proof that it scarcely needed a driver, while we were left to discover ourselves in each other.

Chapter VII

THE HEAT WAVE

WE began, shadows and all, to move on.

The heat of the afternoon, the heat of the blood, the heat of each other—equivalent each to each.

Our hands, little bodies of nakedness, left free as children at play and unashamed, given into one another. The thrust of resolute fingers through the yielding interval of fingers: possessing—possessed.

The first of communions—the communion of hand in hand.

We were passing through a village of tempest-blown people who walked sideways. Spells of fair weather never gave them time to readjust themselves. They tilted to one side or the other like their mud-embedded sail-boats.

The sea and river slimes lodged here. Roots at low tide exposed starfish stuck in their fibres. A fallen birch lays its skeleton between the oncoming tide and the outgoing currents of the estuary: junction of sweet and bitter waters, where the drowned drift down stream, out to sea, or cling to the oozy undercliff.

A wild race of sailors in a few huts live on the eels and sprats, quick as quicksilver, and on the wreckage of ships.

She moralised:

"Those who live by driftwood must needs pray for shipwrecks!"

We had climbed the cliff overhanging a desolate sweep of shore known as the Love-Room.

Throw her over as she leaned to look from the gelatinous mound of half-hardened slime into the abyss of tangled roots and sea-scum beneath?

She must have felt our desire between her propped shoulder blades, for she suggested: "Let us go down."

Two great ribbed hulls rocked together by the wave motion. Soon we, too, would be caught under the cliff—no place in which to linger.

Deep moved wave rollers pounded down the sand, singing at their work, sea-treading it.

Farther along the curved beach a stream mouthed its way through the pebbles and the sand.

Jelly-fish of opaque, star-sapphire blue, outlined it, some with devil-fish tentacles, others bearded, with anguished eyes of the crucified Christ.

Far out, three phantom, or real, shrimp fishers with hunched backs—backs with baskets—gone marketing in the sea, visible and invisible in the hide-and-go-seek of the haze.

We turned from the magics of high noon, subtler than the enchantments of midnight, following a path slippery as fish underfoot, along narrowing alder planted banks of a stream. Rare weeds, too, grew in its earth. High hemlocks grazed our clasped hands:

Palms of love veined like the opal, little maps joining their life-lines.

Our faces broke through spider webs; the things we said as perishable as their silk threads passed between our smiles and the briar roses.

A stopped mill wheel let waters fall peacefully from above, a drift of irruptive bubbles, a twig, registering their imperceptible swiftness, pulverised below into spray.

A brown and white layered manor with gables and wings, farms and granges, the cattle grazing on the salted pasture lands just within sight.

As we looked on another's home, we felt saved from we knew not what suspending danger.

Upon the scorched bank of fern grasses, we drank of the smooth curved sheet of descending water.

Tempering the freshness, she offered her deep mouth to my drinking, then to my stung hand.

Passion, compassion.

Love that women know best.

Love, their escape, shutting off all other discoveries.

Simplified by sensation, would nothing open the intermediate world to her, purify her cadences and decadences?

"On earth as it is in heaven."

Why did she fear new ways of meeting?

Her usual methods gathered us to her surface that we might catch fire rather than light.

She opened her little mirror, reflecting her blaze of hair near ours, fading ours.

She remarked: "My live flame, your ashes."

Having retouched the rouge of her lips, she put a cigarette between them. . . .

Shield her lashes of dark gold and marigold from the match I held for her? Or let its flame catch hold of her crisp hay-loft of hair?

Flay her alive for her indefinite being?

As nothing yet apparent justified this recurring resentment, we found its cause in A.D.'s life before ours with this woman.

As in the presence of a convalescent, she avoided all allusions to that former love-sickness.

Question her?

Interrupt our day to get from her a stale crumb or a false sweetmeat?

Rather trust chance revelations. Not much truth in a woman's answers. She would fit them to fit and flatter herself as she wished to appear. Never destitute enough to feed on bare facts, she would rather dwell with false images, with memory's imagination, reinvent her past?

Detached from A.D.'s experience, we nevertheless felt the pain—the ache of its absence.

Could we not smooth ourselves out, imitate that sheet of water where summer in peace looked on summer, in natural Narcissism?

Already the light was aslant, sawing in two rows of alder trees, topping the bushes with shears soon to be sheathed.

The stream breathed its water-lily, water-melon breath, delivered from the heat.

Sleepy waters ready for their bed, flushed by the sun that had blazed on them all day, now making deposits of a richer gold.

A flash on the surface. The leap of a fish? Too shallow for trout? Her mirror, as it turned, slipping into the water?

To plunge in after her mirror, she took off her flowered muslins that sweated to her close as tattooing. They fell from her, making a flower-bed on the grass, a little fearful at first of standing naked, then reassured by the sight of so many perfect details that must needs put to shame any clothed intruder.

Her body's line uninterrupted by any bathing-suit, her neck, legs and arms no longer amputated by dark interferences, followed their natural sequence to a full-flushed meaning, winning their woman's rights. Her breasts, uplifted centres, where heart and senses unite and exalt each other—no longer closed eyelids of flesh, but remoulded in the glow of the fallen daylight, again they looked at us.

Her joined thighs ready to dive, still held back on the bank with taut toes, the summer ermine of her marked by one dark spot, and three as her arms lifted.

She seemed so glowing, so on fire, that we were surprised not to hear her body singe and sizzle as it met the water.

The water received her with silent chimes, giving out ever-widening circles of vibration.

The trees trembled on their liquid base as she pushed sheets of water over their reflections. Her arms paddled her past the swish of reeds and dimpling water-coils, down through the stream's transparency.

As she disappeared, we quickly undressed and followed Iver through the glaze of azure waters that hid their depth by superposed transparencies.

About to catch and pin her down, we were obliged to return to the surface for breath. We had both swum to where a white barrier crossed the whole end of the pool. How far did this barrier's reflection extend under the water?

To find the mirror, to measure the depth of drowned reflections, our lungs full of new breath we plunged again, swimming between two waters, then downward, until we struck the bottom carpeted with images. An aquatic court?

A dimly-coloured pageantry lay in pomp, pavilion lifted, on the bed of the stream. It was no illusion. She also opened her eyes in the water's midst—eyes hard-boiled past dissolving—instantaneously discerning:

Powdered ladies and gentlemen, their curved backs leaning on consoles; a sceptered queen on a mussed bed-like throne, with a progeniture of cupids caught in the draperies; against a forest of threads, a pastoral scene with lambs; a shepherdess with hooped skirt buoyant with water or uptilted by her shepherd, pretty as a girl, his one hand on her dove-escaping breasts, the other bent on a deeper undoing. Four corner stones held the bordures in place. A drowned eighteenth century taper-lit levy, preserved under glass cover of polished waters, or the manor's tapestries spread out to be cleansed by the current:

A foot to the nearest stone shot us up to the upper world. The barrier still held in the burnished pool.

Why had we not sworn allegiance to the secret court below . . . remained on that bed where queens were more varied in threaded blushes than in this world of setting suns? Tied to the corner stones that had expelled us, we might have swung against each other forever in vain dalliance.

How simplified and poor Nature looked to us after the art-embroidered bowers, garlands, and borders our light swimmers' feet had trod. The surface of the pool, washed grey of prisms and dyes into a nightfall of tin-tones, presented the varnish of a daguerreotype.

We dressed and walked quickly away. Did we fear, more than the sea's Love-Room, the attraction of darkening waters?

Hardly discernible the uniting of trees with their reflections, the exchange of river with road, each becoming the other.

Mists rising from impalpable fields to meet the stars, to be confounded with the milky way.

The twilight . . . ? or was it a forest so thick that the twilight could hardly enter with us?

Great trees, marked with blue-lipped signs, silently suggested a way.

Distinct in the gloaming, a cube of gold: the keeper's lodge? A dog barked.

Curtained in the warm vapour, of similar footfall, we passed by.

A whiff of hay from the meadows. The last round of the hay cart taking off a belated groups of haystacks. Then immersed in the forest to hear and smell its upper sea, the antennæ of branches and leaves searching one another out, touching tips in the dark element. The different warmth of the Glow-woman's cheek on my cheek, the roughness of tweeds against partial nakedness, feet still gliding together on the fern fabrics or stumbling over a tree root's hardened veins.

Her body lunging forward—our hands on her forward hips—a prow-figure—a winged victory? A full sailed ship of sealed treasures?

Manned by us, strong as a male multitude, we pressed on her.

Confessing within ourselves a civil war,

A continuous battle without victory,

A destructive tempest of ill-spent lightning.

Our celestial ardour put to this physical service was so strange to her that she must have thought us mad. Had we astonished and frightened this slave to sexual habits, functioning absent-mindedly and in silence? Reassured, her backward look at us became blind kissing.

Above the tree-crests on a hill an abandoned lighthouse—an empty summer-house? One side, turned full seaward, had been rent away by the spring equinox. A match showed a dead seagull caught in the rafters. Fishing tackle for stream and deep sea fishing lay entangled on a table. A package of mildewed cigarettes, still damp in spite of the heat wave. Bits of candle, pieced together, which the Glow-woman lit and stuck in a shell.

The floor on which we fell together smelt of pine.

To locate desire—a simplification.

But too excited to choose a gesture, we battled, finding no issue to each other.

Surprise her into unwilling pre-nuptial ecstasy— break in through her hand barriers?

Bedded on the wall, our shadow in close mingling with her shadow cut an audacious figure—a pornographic imitation of love-making.

Were we they . . . were they we?

Where joined, where separate?

Lie down, you shadow woman, and beget us darkness, semblances to feed our Shadows on.

The defenceless easy coupling of shadows seemed to mock our efforts.

In shame, in envy, a lifted hand, freed from the struggle, displaced the candle to throw the couple on the floor, where our prone caricature invented other adjustments.

We blew them out with the candle, that they should not imitate the full-sailed belly making for joy in laboured rhythm, measuring the span of a future pregnancy, from which a cry and sterile spasm seemed to deliver?

We staggered to our feet. She lay limply across out arms, losing consistency and structure, carried out into the night.

We stretched her on the ground under the trees. Some stars lit on the branches.

Uncoupled, left alone in our throb, the legion in our blood still claimed her!

The love-rapture, its fall into and rise from the physical, its humiliating sequence, seemed an inadequate substitute for some supreme communion confiscated and sought for through the limited vibrations of flesh.

She came to life with a practical question: "Is the station far? . . .The last train 00.3. How can I walk?"

Her head fell back in a swoon . . . in a sleep?

We breathed between her lips a breath that brought her breath back to ours.

The sound of a cart grated past on the upper road. We ran to try to stop it, and carried our mistress to where the patient horse and willing driver waited. The high cart wheels seemed the wheels of the mill. The road ran as a stream under them—wheeling us on—grinding down our still united shadows.

A warm gust on our face. Someone near, invisible, trying to speak? . . . or the last yawn of the day dropping off to sleep?

The driver sat on the right, leaving thus the seat to us. Tired by the swim, the fear, the mysterious danger, the interrupted joy, she slept, and we were released from her.

Now, she roused herself, wide-awake and separate, uncommunicative, unpossessed, unattainable, in selfish exhaustion that left us no part.

Her after-love, its tenderness, belonged to no one?

She sat far apart, as though fearing our contact, her face thinking elsewhere.

We looked away, relaxing on averages—caring no
more about her.

The cart lanterns, dim as fire-flies,
A-shine on the white mare's hind-quarters.
Under the crisp lifted tail, the india-rubber butt, soiling
    the traces, then closing. . . . . .
A station—an enlarged Swiss clock—edging the forest,
Expectancy on the platform, signals, the song of wires.
Trepidation, inhalation of the vacuum-conquering
    engine,
An invasion of machinery in resonant marrow bones
    and torn ear-drums.
A stop, a dizzy panting steam—a silence.
From without the moving squares of gold light,
From within the peopled stalls,—
A zoo of human animals, many seen before,
Others insignificant enough on first sight.
A keeper moving amongst them fearlessly.
We observe surfaces, aware of little differences,
Counterparts, complexities of the travelling menagerie;
Then, physician-like, probe under the reserve to the
    inner secrets
Discerning hidden diseases and divergences of variety.
Under their appearances, the dominant future,
The yet discreet danger-signals of pent-up animalities,
Dressed and sociable, hindered by bars and chains of
    convention.
To detect the snake-in-the-grass look,
The shaggy lion's timidity,
That Lamia, eliminating the poisons of her fangs

Against the smoky glass of her cage
As she seems to fix an imaginary enemy outside.
That placid eunuch woman freed from her entrails,
The baby with the diaper smell crumpling with wetness
    the mother's pongee dress;
A falcon profile asleep under hood, or ready to prey on
    hunted eyes; . . .
The mastiff dog-faced mother, deserted by her batch;
That bald vulture throwing out a rotten meat smell;
An aged monkey stealthily occupied.
Planning difficult sexual adjustments
As he lusts towards a naked-legged female of five.
The kangaroo woman compressing her pregnant belly,
Her mate, who was he that living consumptive skeleton
    seated beside her;
An electric panther, naked finger-nails glistening
    through her furs;
A dove-like holy ghost of a man with cooing eyes;
That stockbroker, shifting from right to left his crude
    animality,
As an old whore staring at this resumé of male life
Has a reflex opening of the knees,
Her vanity bag in her lap jolts indecently with the
    train's jolts;
The occupants of each stall then rise and are collisioned
    together,
A long line of fornicating overcoats and skirts stagger
    towards the exit,
Warm belly against the one and hot desire pursuing
    another.
They sever and disperse, with looks anxiety, indiffer-
ence or aversion;

A rude haste now forces them apart and out.
They gather again, an obscure line of compact and
    complicity,
While the other keeper confidently opens the turn-gates,
Setting them loose on the city night.
They thin out to single antagonisms of traffic,
Streets difficult to play through as a game of chess,
Each on foot or wheel, making towards a secret room
    of torture,
An isolated motor on lagoon-like side street
Runs over underlying reflections to a quiet quarter.
One kiss between two women lasting from the Gare
    St. Lazare to the Luxembourg Gardens.
A man with protruding teeth and pointed nose ferrets
    his way out to the nearest brothel;
A gas jet makes the walls sweat in the cheap hotel,
While syncopated snores serenade the communicating
    door between,
Through which a line of light and a form of light meet
    at right angles.
A rowing sound denotes the arm's full length stroke of
    brush through a yard of unshorn hair.
Time pulsates on the bed-tables
A beat coupled with the blood.
Wild-eyed cats decipher the moon's disc,
The night's coin pays down ready silver
To see into the nightmares of the sleepers.

We became so easily what we chanced to see, to
sense, divine, imagine, that we had some difficulty in

summoning back our legion. Participating too greatly in others, we felt their sensations instead of our own.

So aware were we of external life that we seemed to lose sight of our own life—just as we see others and are to ourselves but the invisible centres of this observation.

A moment of anguish, of getting back, succeeded this state in which we were neither ourselves nor anyone else,—neither there nor here. So abroad, so lent out, that had anyone addressed us during this interlude, the shock of being found absent might have dispersed us—lost us altogether.

So let us not question the sleep-walker bent in a direction so perilous, of so singular a sanity, that to stand in the way might be to awaken into madness one seeking some mysterious solution—a bridge—an equilibrium on border lines, a blending of the outer and the inner being, to supplant consciousness by some more evolved medium.

We managed to gather ourselves together as the horsecab drew past the Glow-woman's gate. The old coachman in scare-crow clothing remained immovable, as night ran its small hours into the doubled tariff of the taximetre.

The Glow-woman tried to make up for her neglect by a moment of effusion at parting:

"Come in as far as the inner door, will you? When again? Shall we go away to-morrow night for a marriage of two days? "

We had entered the quiet court, passed through the first arches. A light lit up the large glass window.

Someone still waiting for her?

She did not see, or choose to see, though she was careful as a humming-bird to reach just into our nearest ear:

> "You are One desired by One
> Between two settings of the sun—
> If I were I or you were you
> Perhaps for a life or two!" . . .

Her singing lips made the little verses tingle through us. Glad of her finishing touch, she vanished.

As she entered her studio its light increased.

Outside, the ocuba bushes, their slippery leaves splashed with dabs of milk, shared the electric glare that poured over the low sill.

We remained indefinite in the moon-premise, irresolute whether to go or to stay.

To stay and to watch. . . .

To watch and to listen.

Was she alone?

We listened and heard only our own heart.

We shut our eyes, trying to catch some word. . . . Rap at the glass? Ring the bell?

Nothing so obvious matched the shy irresolute night mood, magnifying the importance of each act.

A movement at the heart made us again aware of her. . . . Were we falling in love?

The moments passed with her repeated themselves—a magic-lantern show of our day with her passed over our senses. Why had it ended?

We stood wondering how we had parted . . . why we had parted.

Not until the next night?

Who was to have this love-night prepared by us?

Did we not already know all her passion could not give us? How incomplete is completion!

Our shadow pointed the way out, emphasising that we desired her and wished to remain on the wrong side of our decision.

The sharp sound of the outer gate made us retreat into the thicket, where we crouched, as the steps and jokes of a belated party came near, turning on the electricity in going through the glass doors and upstairs.

We had better go,—who has a right to stay?

Go? Were we not curious of her actions without us? Stay? . . . Jealous?

Go, the voices within us urged, and fear encouraged, flashed out opposing resolutions, both to be obeyed. Two choices, both stinging like the split snake's tongue before the double bite.

We had reached the outer arches when the gate again opened and shut. We had missed our chance of slipping out with the incomer, and had to get behind the big tree against the wall. This time no voices, no group, but a man running headlong. His hat prevented recognition as the window light struck him. He rang at the atelier door—no key? Surely then, a lover? Not the boy-husband? He seemed taller, and why such haste?

He had run to be with her. Or because he was late from someone else and wanted not to appear so? . . . Psychology of the husband? . . . Or desire running towards relief?

We understood something of male psychology; lovers to be served hot.

What a limited intimacy not to know how she is with other lovers.

The key-hole? The eye to the key-hole? Could we stand it?

Cut them apart, with a look . . . a knife?

Surely we had been jealous and eaves-dropping before—many times before. Ah, the weariness in the intensity.

Voices were just audible, but not their tone. Who was he . . . and so late?

We raised ourselves to the familiar sill; it cracked and we dropped again among the ocuba bushes.

To know, to see how another is with another.

Up again on the sill . . . a look in . . . The studio lamp burned as daylight.

Duthiers was there, and she was making up for lost time, working under pressure to finish his portrait.

The boy-husband, screened from them, was preparing for bed—taking off his shirt—his mild eyes looking unseeingly into the space where we watched, inlooking on some pleasant thought.

The trio had something so usual, so familiar, that it broke our mood into insignificance.

But remembering A.D.'s low jealousy confessed in the book—the mutilation to escape, the suicide to retrieve,—we grew afraid of elements we contained that might lead to a like issue.

Rested, refreshed from her, the sting might revive? Jealousy, worse than neuritis, might lead into insupportable pain. . . . Let the nerves sleep.

As we were shut out, so they were shut in. We re-
membered the boy-husband's prayer to us. So we were
to be their remedy, carefully administered, to secure
a better circulation, combustion, exchange—sameness
tempted, through difference, to realise
   itself.
   But what of that automaton posing for her?
   Her part: to tempt and escape—to renew the worn-
out springs of the matrimonial mattress, be given a lift
by us to Paradise regained?
   Jealousy, the love stimulant, had failed. Someone in
us felt cheated, let down, almost disappointed.
   Seeking martyrdom, we had encountered boredom.
We gave a Satanic yawn.
   On the way home we were met by a street-walker
. . . over-ripe bruised fruit no one had picked up.

Chapter VIII

IN A.D.'S LIBRARY

WE awoke not knowing where nor who we were. Having lost touch with consciousness and unconsciousness that pass on the work of the one to be finished by the other.

We felt fresh from nowhere, dispossessed, free.

Sleep, the dark room where we develop negatives—snapshots of the preceding day, deformations grotesquely recognisable.

Dreams, the go-betweens, had gone nowhere, left no imprint.

Even our dreams had fallen to sleep—or had we fallen to sleep in a dream?

Sand-man, jester, peddler transforming old wares into new before our closing eyes.

Conjuror, changing us and the objects about us into something else.

Messenger, why did you go past our door leaving no message?

Prodigal, reformed into virtue and poverty.
Stay-at-home, where are your wanderer's gifts?

In our sleep-drugged eyes no mirage of your
upside-down world of reversed lenses:

Where each act is separate and without
consequence;

Where cause, a poor relation to effect, is not
received;

Where nakedness passes, unnoticed, in a crowd.

And explosives are silent.

And the murderer is an innocent child-faced
giant.

Within or without a dream, we soon became aware
of our stage-setting, the part we had been playing.

Playing a part suggesting that we belong to a whole?

This fixed reality destroying the chance of the Real.

Because of the obstacles of this set of realities, we
should perhaps never find our Reality!

We did not remember a door opposite our bed—

A door left open. . . .

Someone had gone from us?

Or someone had entered during our sleep .

. . . Been watching our sleep. . . .

. . . Taken us from our sleep, gypsied us away.

Too late to pursue on the heels of mystery, turning
round an angle into a dimension beyond?

The next room empty.

Empty?

Our naked feet walked on water-cool marble.

Marble, the veined flesh of Venus?

We had come to a blind issue, found ourselves in a library from which there was no exit.

Books lined the four sides.

Books closed in the door through which we had entered.

No plaster walls reflecting shadows.

Here we should exchange our shade for the definite little shades thoughts leave on paper.

Paper, the mind reader.

Paper, the virgin of receptivity, the white priestess, had confessed all those who now stood bound on the shelf.

High-backed folios gave the impression of organ pipes.

Their radiation, vibration, atmospherical stillness, was so intense that to one who could play collectively on so collective an instrument, instantaneous knowledge of their capacity followed a look at them.

They never need be displaced or tried by one who knows how not to read.

To feel what's in a book is better than to learn it by heart.

We perceived from the vantage-ground of so many unopened books that most were written through some disease. An irritation in the brain, fermenting ideas that lead to religions and revolutions, actioning a maddened strength; for not only individual action, but the actions of multitudes had been prepared in these quiet places of the mind.

Few had been emancipated from their organisms— pure secretaries receiving supreme dictates.

Which, of so many writers, had A.D. preferred?

The fevered, the torpid, the consumptive, the consuming, the visionary, the insane? The seeing, the far-seeing, the inspired?

Those who wrote with their soul, their bile?

Those who wrote with their blood, or the blood of others?

Were not these books the imposed ancestors of A.D.'s mind? Or had they been chosen after the years of formation, the atavistic transmitting of tastes and tendencies, or revealing tastes and tendencies already habitual?

We approached the nearest shelves, where a curious order had been kept.

The books a little above the eye level were mostly the books of poets: poets who gave off a feeling of their rich blood.

Above our heads ranged books of superhuman vision. Some of these joined those poets who saw with the eye of the forehead degenerated into the penial gland.

Books of thought—inspired thought—were also found in this section, evolved beyond the ego, having laid self apart, using it merely as a scribe of their visions.

Then came the confessions of lovers and other martyrs, and the sentences of ironists who had taught their wounds to smile.

In opposition to these, followed books of cold observation of a realism so exterior that it was more obvious what their authors had let slip than what they had captured.

The novels, treating of the affairs of the heart, at the place of the heart.

Erotic anthologies joined them below this vital region. A.D. considered pornography nothing but eroticism badly written and deserving no quarter.

The mediums of modernism as mannequins of fashion, were also excluded, because an acquired speed can never represent a movement. Documentary pamphlets and other statistical swindles, with every fact warped to prove a point—truth, that Might-Be, bent out of shape to fit a preconceived idea—and encyclopedias big with inexact precisions, and volumes of philosophy records of the successive errors of the human intelligence, were abandoned to the level of our feet.

We were impressed less by the bibliographical rarity of some of the books, than by their variety which, though it seemed to exclude predilection, betrayed A.D.'s peculiar character by the rather arbitrary arrangement.

Aware of their importance as a mass, only a few detained us by the generating forces they supplied to others.

What a lot of printed matter contained within the measurements of a body.

. . . And its influence might extend through as many generations as the vices of the blood.

Such-and-such a book had perhaps called us into existence?

What books produced you? might be asked as conclusively as—Who are your parents?

Chance and choice were also ruled out of the laws of intellectual inheritance.

We touched the shelves and our ribs. What books had passed from them into us? become part of our make-up?

Are we not each a circulating library spreading ideas, dreams, precepts, social and scientific prejudices—the first-hand work of some writer? That writer the writer of another; most inspiration merely unconscious plagarism, and writing in general a moment of arrested development; for what is an opinion but a full-stop in our comprehension to be passed on through print without end?

The shelved room, the cellular and ribbed organism, were but the contribution of a contribution?

Might we not at least get ourselves into the order of a well distributed library, assigning to each a place?

The morning, with its practical arranging energy, put to shame the chaos in which we found everything concerning us. For though we knew many things, we knew almost nothing of our own representations.

We must first give rank to our invading legion, who had showed, on several occasions, a disregard for discipline, precedence and hierarchy.

We sat down at the table that occupied the middle of the library. The light falling from an equally long transom diffused itself on to some foolscap writing-paper.

We must choose a system of classification—make our inventory, determine our composite. Establish an order where each might exist and serve.

Put down every wanderer found in our catacombs, fix them by some familiar trait, and so learn to know and govern our ghosts, our lovers, our low-characters, our martyrs and saints, and any that we might encounter in this journey through ourselves. Surprised that authors had established no manner of dealing with even their fictitious personages, should we not definitely adopt the play-writer's method of giving a name to each *dramatis persona*—the drama here consisting in their divergences and conflicts—their combined chemistries. But what of their simultaneous claims and antagonisms?

Rather treat them as a musical composition? Draw up a list of instruments to be conducted, and decide which is to give tone value to our design. We began ruling a page before us like an orchestral score. This form would allow us distinctness and unison. We would register what was voicing us as a conductor registers cunningly the effect of each sound.

How now orchestrate ourselves? Group our faculties as a composer groups the different sonorities by which he is to be interpreted? Let them respond, cover the voices of each by each, and find in just opposition their balance—in union their unity?

Had we no soloist to put to the fore? Imposing a voice above the massed voices?

To give both individual and collective significance to the development, as the Greek chorus answers the single interpreter by the collective expression.

We must at least record this—and each one rising momentarily to this, emphasise a crescendo of single sound, wave a whisper into silence. So each would, in turn, assert its phrase and fall back into the partition.

Should no one sing continually above the others? Carry the score into pure song?

Every time a new voice suggested itself, we entered it, as a musician might add a hautbois to his composition.

But the weak point of such a rendering appeared in the unregisterable material—a buzz, a haze, intermingling the lines where one was hardly distinguishable from the other.

This discouraged our orchestral attempt. Such nuances could only be inscribed on the blended bars of a rainbow!

Exorcists must have encountered just this difficulty in driving out devils that would hide and cling together and defy selection.

Instead of imitating slavishly the system of another art, we would amuse ourselves by using the great variety of lettering, and each character would have its corresponding character in print:

Capitals serve for soul declaration;

The Elzevir for the Romantic;

The Grasset type for the sensual and emotional.

Italics, as usual, for everything that is, or seems, a quotation—and all state fixtures of sensation.

The difficulty read Gothic would be reserved for poetry—at best almost hermetic, its illuminations a flowering of the blood giving us a semblance of the gorgeous world that pulsates within twisted arteries.

Anonymous observations in journalistic print.

Marginal notes for single, or outside, observations.

Dashes, and dashes combined with dots, and dots with dots, for passages relating to sexual intercourse, as usual in English.

The retrospective could be dealt with in backhand, the prophetic in forehand, the shadings to indicate nuances.

So our faculties marked down in different types and scripts would be quickly distinguished, and as easy to recognize as differently dressed individuals in a thoroughfare.

Identified rather by the silhouette given by the letters than by the nomenclature. But in seeking to put each down as in a directory:

Who's who
And
Whose whose

we again realised that such inventions are irksome, and diminished by application. We dropped into a meditation on the origin of composite beings in general; on the duality of mind characterizing several persons in one; on an entity at variance with one of its selves, hoping in this way to throw a better light on our difficult case.

Fatigued by our mania for classification, we found ourselves envying the single being—be it but a snail—its coupled animalism dominated by a succession of single wants.

Then we became enchanted by the dual being—the centaur—part man and part beast; the siren—the sphinx, rising half woman and half wave; from the animal into the human mystery.

The Egyptians "double,"—the two faced Janus, the two-sexed hermaphrodite.

And on another plane, the angel, the double-being guardian over the human duality.

> A double being needs no other mate—
> So seraphita-seraphitus lives:
> Self-wedded angel, armed in self-delight,
> Hermaphrodite of heaven, looking down
> On the defeat of our divided love.

Following on this too happy state, the separate pair creative of a third, their three dimensional perception, their godhead a trinity.

The three-in-one leading to four: out of the third the fourth.

The blur of mystery still clinging to it—Mystery: a spent Truth out of focus, or that which is not yet, the forerunner of occurrence?

To stretch the mind beyond its present possibilities may be to indicate a place towards which it will ultimately travel to the further discovery of itself.

Gods, masters, and libraries for their advertisement, are instituted for the incomplete, whose imperfect vision must be helped; the complete, or completed, not to be interrupted in their solitary communing by those outside themselves, bequeath books to answer for them.

Moses, the law giver, consulted but the god within him—gave commandments to the tribes of Israel that he might be left in peace—and outside the gates of the promised land. Christ, overshadowed by his dark companion, refused to be tempted by the world before him. "Get thee behind me, Satan!"

The voices of Saint Joan were "HER VOICES," and her prayer called into service the warrior of triumph and defeat, and her Saint, within her, who led her beyond all her victories.

Composites of many evolutions reached a prototype, a finality in the Buddha—aware of his every lived life, and dupe no longer of any of them.

Evolutions, first successive then simultaneous,—in the one being—leading to liberation:

"The one to oneness returning."

So, without knowing the incidental experiences, we had learnt A.D.'s lesson.

We would no longer seek to co-ordinate, but to liberate ourself from the legion, and find in their midst the lost leader, the one they had silenced.

Our mind enjoyed a oneness, a well-being, a soaring, an insight, a conquering precision; we would have been loath to have interrupted by riotous opposition.

Enriching uniformity, dictates of a concentrated and developing force, had given us our high commandment. Abstractions now moved as freely through us as the world of images. We had graduated from sensation into a higher sense.

Thought, an immaculate conception, had no use left for the imperfect medium of our body.

After this flight, borne up on the heavy wings of books, how should we return, accomplish our mission, be "present" in the story we had fallen into?

Chapter IX

OTHER DISCOVERIES

A S we went back into the other room the dumb-waiter revolved.

The physical world claimed us, and we fell, faint with hunger, upon our lunch.

The letters had been transferred from the breakfast to the lunch tray, which held out to us:

Hors d'oeuvres— mostly vegetable: stripped radishes, the undefended hearts of artichokes that give to a drink of water their after-taste.

Saddle of spring lamb which our appetite rode to the end, making but a mouthful of its kidney steeped in mint-sauce.

Money affairs offered in large print to tempt the eyes of capitalists: the experienced, weary, far-sighted eyes of fifty.

A bunch of press clippings criticising A.D.'s last book of poems: *Poèmes*. A quotation ran:
Marques, mais marques
    en maitre,
L'étre méritant d'étre,

Sois celle qui pénètre
Sous l'écorce et s'inscrit
Aux seves de l'esprit
Dont ton nom se nourrit;
L'empreinte cérébrale
Grandit comme s'étale
L'arbre et l'initiale. . . .

Great melliferous peas
Amour, left to sail in
their pods to a melting
maturity.

Amour, sport qui nous
    nuit,
Mais sans lequel s'ennuient
Les princes de la nuit.
Princesse à pierre fondre,
Daignez vous descender
Dans ce pays du tendre?

And we were struck
back by:
The night that was for me
    is for him,
And lovers are made over
    like old clothes
To fit new shapes—
. . . And you walk on the
    hearts of those buried
    alive.

Salad, with delicate
herbs: a pasture in a plate.

Coeur à la crème: faint
heart of a little Trianon.
    Fruit (which we left
untouched), for the best
comes last, and we are
wasted on lesser Edens.

And what a parting
was commemorated by:
The sinister gap of wharf-
    water widens
—Slice of an abyss.
The braids of rope thrown

back
Freed from the irons spool.
No human leap can now
    reach
The sickening heart-beat
    more real than life!
Weeping faces, rained on
    like glass,
Glass faces transparent
    with distance,
In the breeze the touch of
    invisible hands,
Linen still waving its
    single winged farewell.

Coffee, bitter exalta-
tion, soothed by a glass
of Alicante.

Satisfied with our lunch and with the poet we we
read through an entire sonnet:

Shall we close our horizon on a few?
Draw little circles round a mortal head?
Give immaterial gold its weight in lead?
Disdain those others for the one or two?
Intrinsic metal should its worth renew
To hold us fast through many a bridal bed,
Be found again, and loved and comforted,
Remint our halo in a ring for you?

Drowned rings an ever widening ring shall bear
Upon the vibrant waters—spheres of air
But shape the bell into distended sound.
However we may go upon our round
—Did the night-watchman take away your veil?—
Our song of songs must in the end prevail.

The criticisms, as usual, cancelled one another.

The poem, *Sadisme Salutaire*—diamond against diamond—which we had already read, quoted in someone's letter the previous morning, was here taxed with obscurity—a rather serious charge for a diamond.

The same critic took to task for too much clarity and simplicity a little dirge:

> Just as she drew us near
> Too soon did she repel
> Us from her flowered bed.
> Again upon her bier
> —A flowered bed as well—
> The doleful crystals fell
> From out my eyes, a well
> That never dried-up be
> Lest in seeing, we see
> Her dead!

If the great sorrows are expressed with puerility, it proves that, undone by grief, we drop into forms that hearts have been broken into since the first. It requires a cool head to create a new medium of expression. A.D. seemed to have lost that mastery.

We all cry more or less in the same manner.

A thick letter accompanied this printed matter of the second morning's post.

Were we to sit down every day to this bureau-work of opening A.D.'s letters?

The envelope contained several pages, evidently from a gentleman proud to be on writing terms with dead languages:

Classic quotations, Greek "e's" were everywhere conspicuous. Nervous shadings and twists, and emphatically barred and prolonged letters, betrayed unusual stress in a script otherwise steadied by years of application and print-clear.

This lengthy letter contained a perfumed page.

—Where had we breathed that perfume before?

A woman's interlaced writing opened its delicate designs between the margins.

Decipher this lingerie?

With difficulty we read, and were charmed in reading:

> A *faux pas* may be the first Step of a dance. . . . Recommend such an example as mine in our world where no one dare move, our friends all being caught in one another's laughter.

No sooner had we entered into communication with these spirit tracings than we felt led up to and locked out of a mystery belonging to us, and looked to the scholarly hand for the key and directions:

> I've hesitated to write to you, but to whom else should I address my condolences over our mutual loss?
>
> Because you are a living legend, and because I am singularly aware of the intimate anarchy of such

a life as yours, my hesitation would have balanced over to the side of the silent and conventional oppressor, had I not, in looking over Stella's affairs, come across a package of letters which you returned to her after a misunderstanding—a misunderstanding I found it easy to bring about and perpetuate. Proud natures believe anything that gives sufficient pain, so I was able to destroy a happiness which I was unable to win.

I belong to a race in which fire has become extinct, but to get fire is my great preoccupation. *Cupiditatum incendio inflammatus.* Though I never have been able to procure in myself the torrification where pure gold is wedded to pure gold, still, I am a passable goldsmith, shaping It to serve my designs. Let us fear most of all, those who are without fire; who act on principle—the source of all deformations.

A gentleman of leisure must have some sport during the winter months in the city (*formosissimus annus*), and I've found the hunting of women at least as diverting as riding to hounds, though the spurred ardour of the start has rarely allowed me to be in at the finish.

Nevertheless, the chase of rare game has been worth the exercise of faculties long since excluded from public affairs by a bourgeoisie of organized mediocrity. Our game—the only game left an aristocracy who lost their head some centuries ago—is to spike victims of as good a quality as possible on our points: a crown has become a very empty hat! *Mais un chapeau fort pointilleux.*

The duel between us—a duel to the death—is over as far as this affair is concerned, so I lay down my arms, for we have both lost!

My orders were necessarily cruel when, after Her illness, you came in a demented state to my official door and were told by the butler:

—"Madame vient de mourir."

My marriage conventions ceased with Her death, and Her burial took place, therefore, as She had willed it—far from our mortuary chapel, with those she called "the real dead."

As She died according to my wishes, you may have found Her again according to yours.

To me of the Positivist school, *une dalle n'est q'une dalle*. About Hers I made this concession because you were both forced to make so many leading up to it—and that I might at last try to learn what they cost.

You who are nearer to Her than Her nearest of kin, forgive the presumption of this stranger: her husband.

I enclose the first of the epistolary liaison found under lock in Her Boulevard St. Germain apartment, and ask you to let me give you the rest, which I dare neither keep nor destroy.

Though I have only met you three times;

When She left me—
When She left you
The night of your suicide and revival.

(I do not count to-day's detour, when you again got in my way)—I am not likely to see you again or at any rate not alone, so beg that you will arrange a meeting in which I may acquit myself of this post-mortem duty.

This request is peremptory: I never discuss, for discussion supposes equality. I am hardly more loquacious than you are. *Silentio et tenebris animus alitur.*

As I wish to preserve a vacuum between these different episodes, I shall continue to appear indifferent and never touch on any subject vital to me when others are present. As you will recall, the letters in question are too intimate to be confided to the post, or to any other than your most obedient servant, Duthiers.

P.S.—And now let us turn over the page and deal with our present bone of contention.

Husbands are only half-men, they cannot *prevent* but only *spoil.* You know this, and that you are a serious disturbance, and again standing between me and what I have chosen to desire. One of us must give way, and I suggest that on this occasion it be you.

I followed the Glow-woman on to your premises the other night more to provoke a solution between us than to make use of the petty sacrilege she suggested by inviting us to sup on that doubly rival tomb. (I deplored the doubtful taste of her Pneumatique, and wish to assure you that I had no active part in it.)

I have abandoned the idea of getting rid of you, of destroying you a second time in *corpore vili*, for you have been killed already and it seems to do you no harm.

I now propose a pact. I give, donate, devise and bequeath the past, which is your domain, with everything appertaining to it: all Stella's belongings at the time of her death, her apartment full of relics and memories, even to "her flowered bed," and promise by this Will not to contest legally, as I have a right to, her place of burial—which in a moment of weakness I forebore to oppose—as long as you leave the present to me. You understand to what present I here allude. "Let the dead bury their dead"—be buried with their dead, and as your lamentations have become public, let them prove consistent.

Thanks to your poetical indiscretions, the whole world knows of your liaison with my former wife. It is now for you Her "rose and golden knight" to give Her your arm for the difficult intermediate state to which She preceded you. She has dearly expiated Her love of you, and deserves you *ad libitum*. May you read in this humour the enclosed letter, which suggests an unending liaison, and which, if we are agreed, no one shall hence-forward prevent.

What Duthiers offered in ironical revenge, we accepted with our whole over-soul.

As the most poignant of possessions the once familiar handwriting of our dead woman:

How magical your pavilion last night. It merited the swift and solitary visit I paid it. It was cut sharp against the diffused night. Only the vigilant light burned in the entry, for what god of love and silence?

By chance I lost—probably on the steps of your front door—a fan of lace and ivory,—a thing of such lightness that I hope it did not trip up the feet of some nocturnal visitor. But I am not sure of the exact place where it fell—this belonging of mine— on my way to you. I do not know what may take place tomorrow, nor do I wish to know. It would have been wiser not to attract me.

Au revoir, my rose and golden knight. Am I to love you? You who are easy to capture, hard to detain, impossible to keep. Why are you not with me now? How go to you? . . . I would take you with me through the warm night to the graveyard in the Bois de Boulogne, that forest in Paris.

So in the beginning and at last She had come to claim us. Had She not come back to us Herself, fan in hand, and no one could shut Her out.

We put the fan and letter, already united by the same scent, together in our breast pocket—a sorrow of tears under our coat—and went out.

And the twilight sang: *J'ai pardonné.*

Ah, dead woman, our love, remote enough for love—for love that is two-thirds regret.

And as we wept the nascent stars rushed together and were blurred and fell from our eyes.

CHAPTER X

INTERFERENCE

A T the distant end of the Longchamps Cemetery the guardian's wife was feeding her ashen brood.

On recognizing us, she smiled the smile expectant of a generous fee. It widened out through the slot of her ruined mouth. By rows of decayed tombs, seated on one of the slabs, the guardian himself presided over the underground dormitory, his little face framed in circles of flesh.

Age doth make eunuchs of us all.

A last whiff of twilight rose from his pipe.

The shadow-people were winning the day over three dimensional appearances.

Faithful as a dog to the place from which our Mistress had disappeared, on the trace of our sorrow we had caught up to our lost life that was no longer a stranger to us, asking in vain to be recognized.

Could we not pray, simply as a child:

"Now I lay me down to sleep?"

For some of us have faith.

"Flirting with death," the Glow-woman said, as she approached through the gloom the most vivid of painted mouths.

The fury in our mind stood high. In answer to our hesitant look, she stammered her excuses:

"I was worried. . . . You did not answer my voice, no one answered, and you did not come to fetch me. So I knew I should find you in this haunt. I cannot lose you, I cannot afford to lose you. Your need of me has become my necessity of you.

"Blond strength that I exasperate, try out, and force, against which I struggle, jealous at its perfection, at its constancy.

"How you hover over and try to protect Her, even here. Wasted away below the earth, a phantom, dragging you down step by step. She is the love of your life. How you still love Her is a mystery; but I shall drive you away, you shall not join Her easily. Each time you come in search of Her you shall find me instead. I make you promises more alarming than any betrayal? Come away with me, come away with me now!

"Willing or unwilling, you loved me once. Have you forgotten our day and play together? . . . Hear the words pounding through me. A million to one of these that get caught into breath. I hold it back lest it branch into fire.

"It is strange to be hurt by your eyes. You are trying to make a crime of our past. Your heart-biting silences . . . the cheapening of pleasure to your disdain. . . . Arched lips arching up into pride. . . . Clumsily, heavily, I fall on you to crush the lyre-like smile. You turn your head your mouth breaks and twists.

"Beauty, my beauty, why bearest thou beauty sadly?

"Open your arms wide when I come falling into them.

"You want other arms than those about your neck. No stretched arms can reach high enough? Do not turn away. A fire is beating in the heart of the rock.

"Throw your cruelty about me like a cape. Give birth to me, I am a changeling thing under your hands."

She tried to gather us back to her, to wrap us in her poor beauty.

The desire we were at a loss to feel had passed into her—become her desire of us.

"Again the fine horses throwing themselves against granite walls, shattering their foreheads' stars, eyes staring blood-struck, at last struck!"

We loathed this insulting frenzy—her want of us. Are not all wants an illusion of the silver-eyed senses?

We could not well evade a situation so strenuously prepared for us. So fortified in another, no interference mattered. We would be patient. Time was as nothing.

When would silly indignation of mind boiling with blood become acts of force?

She would be made to pay dearly for gaining her point now.

To follow her was to act a lie; yet how often only a lie can make the truth clear!

Her shadow imposed her entire masked body against ours along the wall.

A red taxicab received and jolted us together. To the chauffeur she named the Gare de Lyon.

"I chose that station because it has several Southern lines. Shall we go to the South of France? La Savoie? Italy?"

Feeling that she had not won us to her, but that in following her we were following some other purpose, she became prudent, attempted only external eloquence. Her inspiration was spent; she imitated it, exaggerated her effects, played a losing part, rather than no part at all—her last chance.

As though she must somehow carry her audience with her, she resorted to variations on:

"Kennst du da Land?"

Ostentatiously as the coloured pictures posted up in waiting-rooms, she presented:

"La Grande Chartreuse—After the closing hour we can bribe the anti-clerical guardian to allow us to spend the night in one of the monastery's ten thousand hard lust-haunted beds. Or in Madame de Warens' replete eighteenth-century moth-eaten alcove at 'Les Charmettes,' to which Rousseau walked back from Switzerland to find himself replaced by the gardener, and signifying no more to his hostess than a cherry in the time of cherries. Or if Romanticism is too worn a proximate, shall we gather from our own spent force a honeymoon, and return to Normandy, inhabit a 'folie,' mildewed with dampness, on the Côte de Grâce, with only three rooms and an alley of tilleuls through which we can just see the estuary?

"But we have passed the Gare St. Lazare, so we will let the Gare de Lyon suggest where to go."

The word "go" was reminiscent of travel-bent couples who never seem to "arrive," "to go" or to be "on the go" being the great affair.

To practice evasion, the caprice of escape, and by foreign environment to give ourselves the slip, to cut our own acquaintance.

Only to be caught in the first hotel mirror—go towards that stranger—concede, through platitudes of recognition:

"So there you are!"

Extend a hand to an identical hand under glass:

"So pleased to meet you . . . your face is familiar, we seem to have met before"—(formalities, manners, to conciliate this vis-à-vis, however superficial).

"Won't you come in? Just a sham door separates us. I am quite alone. I am sorry I have nothing to offer you."

Travel, the severing of self from self, to end in this fiasco encounter. Inoculation not successful—interrupted, intercepted, on our way elsewhere.

Broken in, brought back, for we all come back, unchanged except for the worse.

The Glow-woman persevered in her refrain, nor interrupted the old song even to take a breath. What did she fear would catch up if she should stop?

"Dahin! dahin! möcht' ich, mit dir o mein Geliebter, ziehn."

Swayed by the general clichés of uninventive lovers she dared suggest: "Venice!" We could stop at the Palazzino of propitious friends whose hall, a continuation of the lagoon, has a waterlapped iron gate rusted open. A bed awaits us there, on the water-level floor—as conspicuous as the beds where kings are conceived and born. A dazzle from the water-changes revives so rigid a pomp, and ripplings on the frescoed ceilings animate the painted goddess whose bosoms heave as shadows play with them. The slightest tempest blows open the windows, but high-back chairs endike currents of air, and a hooded gondola is always ready to knife its passage under the low bridge of the canalletti.

Or we could motor-boat to the Lido, past the mad-houses for Armenians, women and priests. Take leave of Venice, the old queen in her sitzbath, with all her jewels on!

"Or shall we undertake the thrice-broken journey to African Capri, Tiberius's island, too large for one, and soon too small for two? But let us not stay long enough for the figs to become tasteless or the mosquito lose its sting, nor for you to offer a human sacrifice by throwing me over the Tiberius Rock after the Venus and Virgin joint festa.

"Shall we never stand high enough to dive deep enough?"

She looked furtively at us, and then returned to the safer ground of generalisations.

"After experiencing fevered nights of tossing one side to the other of the bridal net, between the paregoric and the citronella—go down to a deserted cove and lie in the sun after bathing in the sea. There are rocks under the surface like the flaws in an emerald, and foot-stools of seaweed to rest on, or push away from, in a race to the horizon, and darkened rooms and rounded roofs and minarets to sing an azan to the sun disk rolling behind Ischia—a prayer of thanks that the cricket has finished grinding its metal into sparks of noise. . . . And say good-bye to each other, if not after the first, at least before the last time!

"Or let us go only half-way South—as we are forced to half-measures—put in near the old port of Marseilles, where sailors land in six strides from their bunks to a prostitute's bed more ready to satisfy their prayers than the Madonna in her tinselled niche.

"During the Allied occupation, we watched one of these bedrooms on the street open and close, thirty times a day, its ardent chapel on men of all religions and colours. These women have solved the problem of how not to stay long enough in an action to be caught in it."

The verbal erotic, victim to her thyroids, continued:

"The next best thing is to be a continual runaway, to outstrip every trap in this chase with the bloodhounds! The wife is a dupe to repetition without variety—asphyxiated with virtue, a fainting figure, receptive of her husband only—the help-mate feeding on her vitals according to his appetite, and he will not even help about the leak in the stove.

"Adultery, our dull alternative. . . . Give pleasure to that Pierrot banjoing on a moon that is not bright enough to discover even our bed-slippers—so why get up to let him in?

"Lovers are but disguised second husbands."

It was evident that this man-inhabited woman had run away on an impulse, actioned less by us than by dissatisfaction at home. She justified her elopement to herself by affirming:

"I put my faith in you to find new delights in this flesh-bare function that, until yesterday, had never fired me—carried me away from it.

"I am half virgin to pleasure, and this is my first real honeymoon."

As she said so, she blushed, not as a virgin, but as an iron ready for striking.

We stood inside the station, in the "hall of lost footsteps." We confronted the twelve clocks pointing to the different hours of departure of trains at the head of each line. The one that matched the present hour advertised: "Dijon, Aix, Chambery, Modane, Turin, Rome."

"Let us take this train if there is a *wagon-lit* left."

The porter had only the best two out of couches in the *lit-salon*.

A black-bearded man—did his beard go way down? gleamed inviting eyes and teeth us from his couch nearest the passage. While she was hesitating about sharing the compartment with him, the train, scheduled to leave at 9.13, started, precipitating us into the *lit-salon*.

As the Glow-woman subsided between us, our travelling companion, dusky and uncontrolled as a Maharajah, shot his eye-balls out of a garniture of crisp hair at her, and left them fixed on her through the sleeper's electric light turned moon-dim.

So to some she was still beautiful, existing mostly as men appraised her.

How we revolted against her insistent red hair! How we despised her for not being the Beloved!

The train's monotonous rhythm forced its hearers to sleep, its motion coupling unconscious bodies to invisible possessors. The Glow-woman jolted, profoundly shaken; the lidless eyes, revulsed in sleep or in ecstasy, still keeping their white hold on her.

A night-sharpened cry broke from the man, rudely awakening us. The Glow-woman turned a shade paler, as though the veins had received a nacreous fluid, and her hand went out in search of ours.

Through the slit in the curtain a station light circled gold rings around her fingers.

The man, now resenting his dream, retreated into the toilet room between compartments, and amongst other adjustments was heard clearing out his throat for the required difficulties of speech.

The Glow-woman whispered:

"It is almost daybreak, we must be nearly somewhere—where? Let us get out!"

The lamps were turned off as day, dressed in grey travelling clothes, came to greet us, and grew brilliant as we sat outside at one of the buffet's little marble tables. We ordered coffee with milk, and as it was too early for fresh bread, she asked for a poached egg. It was brought under-cooked. At the same moment the sun, through its white substance, presented a perfect yolk.

As we walked up the main street, the Bath Establishment was just opening to Bath chairs, carrying in to their treatment those disabled by greed.

Stopping at one of the flower-stalls, the Glow-woman chose a white rose that still clung to blighted dozens wrapped in newspaper in their wicker basket. Taking off the thorns, she slipped it into the button-hole of our coat.

"A white rose for my bridegroom elect!"

Then she disappeared into the post-office—proba-bly to telegraph her habitues that we had decided to go up on the mountain.

The funicular railway tracks, like the backs of two knives, pressed down through the vineyards.

We shuddered as we ascended. Was it already snow-chilled air?

The Glow-woman sat opposite, in the sharp morn-ing. We looked at her mouth.

Everyone was looking at her mouth. Her brilliant naked mouth should be hidden as the sex of her face. As unconsciously she smiled on us, we turned aside for shame.

At the half-way halt, a girl in slim black slip was leaning over a fountain, intently washing out a piece of linen.

—"Ma mère ne croira jamais."

As the funicular almost grazed her, shall we pass her through an arm as a scarf through a ring?

"Maidenhood, maidenhood, where have you gone?"

Next spring, not able to get her through the chapel door.

Had the Glow-woman never thought of sup-planting mankind through child-bearing?

120

Two negatives seeking development through each other.

The mother and child framed apart——a sanctification.

An eagle circled down to the lowlands in search of prey.

Finally, the mountain hotel appeared, a canopy on the top of a kneeling elephant. The funicular laddered us up to it. From the threshold the land-lady informed us that there was no room left but a turret—a four-windowed room which would give us, at any rate on a clear day, the command of the four cardinal points.

The morning lay pillowed on clouds.

"To-morrow we will have a nice free double bed-room," she added, by way of apology, as she led us into the little turret where had been stored everything that no one wanted:

A spotted divan.

A high-railed child's bed enveloped in a mosquito net—hardly long enough for an adult.

A three-legged table.

A bottomless chair.

A clock without hands.

A polychrome bust of Napoleon Barbiche reigned over these mutilated pieces of furniture, irreverently balanced near the mantelpiece by an eidelweiss under a glass globe:

> Oh, flower of the crystal North,
> The cold augments as you star forth.

"In the meantime we shall come across better rooms out-of-doors, and less our-of-doors than staying in this observatory," the Glow-woman went on consolingly, as was her wont, covering her disappointment under bowery descriptions:

"Some will have ceilings of sensitive leaves, and running streams instead of these discouragingly heavy pitchers of water. Nature has more comforts to offer than the average French hotel, and the moss and heather can spread out the better bed.

"Were it not for the clouds drifting in through the windows, making all our room their passageway, the glare here would be terrible. Shall we draw the curtains and order lunch for mid. day?

"Or let us go for a long walk and take our lunch as we find it in some farm. . . . This way, will you? . . . Down towards the meadow-lands?

"I dislike views, nothing to be done with them! Though Nature has only a few clichés repeated over and over again, it can at least refresh, rest, hide, exercise, exhilarate us.

"These pine-woods have a memory that my nostrils quiver to. I, too, associate, am romantic, since I care for you. Here at least we shall not be seen—artists have to be. careful of their reputations. Only people like you—and there is no one like you, darling—can afford to have the best of bad reputations. You are your own public; you depend upon no one, wear no one's name unbecomingly."

Did women generally go on like this? Being desired gave them confidence to try their worst effects. How did she not sicken with the insignificance of the things that mattered to her—become poisoned by her own futile atmosphere?

She was bent upon art—"not to have it live by her, but to live by it." Strenuous, not towards its development, but in the exercise of expedients. Her calculated haste to finish Duthiers' portrait for some exhibition, to rush without piety from this into that, to illumine no day on fine vellum, allow no proper margins.

How she had buckled down to evidences, brought herself to accept them as essential!

The rarest thing in youth is youthfulness.

Her superficiality, ice fragile, over the feelings she created, allowed her to glide above their abyss. No extension outside of herself by which to grasp secrets of her making.

A spiritual dumbness had clouded about her, through which she raised too high a voice.

With so little of us at all versed in the matter, so aloof, so alone, so uncommunicable, she yet forced herself to skid on.

"I am so glad to be again alone with you. . . .

Are you glad to be with your bride of to-night?"

Promised to another bride "through many a marriage bed," we touched the treasure at our aide. As we did so, the white rose separated into petals.

"What an answer!" the Glow-woman said, so sorrowfully that she became almost real.

Make a destiny for her, or let events take the haphazard shape of her behaviour?

Leave her to moods, her masters, instead of becoming her master—the manager of her sensations.

If we followed A.D.'s propensities, how should we revenge them? Can one revenge propensities? Not only a grammatical, but a spiritual impossibility.

We felt what A.D. had certainly felt and fought against in this woman, along with fragments of love set off to worst advantage in a patchwork of oppositions. Her love, a Cubist painting,—perhaps many things there, but chopped up and unrecognisable.

To serve our friends we must espouse their cause rather than their entity—add a delightful force, breeze in to their inextricable situations to get them out of their grooves?

Had we not rather gotten ourselves into their grooves?

Those who fight, fight under the false colours of friendship to their own ends. So A.D. would have us both revenged?

God and the right cause are ever taken into some such compromise.

We have all met with this woman in the flesh, who exists but in the flesh. Lucky if we have not sacrificed a whole existence to her, since any of our subordinates would suit her better. Let them enter this Venusberg in our stead. Women who are too beautiful can offer but a set of stereotyped realities—one can teach them nothing, learn nothing from them; and what is such beauty but an accepted average? Break it for having attracted, misled and detained us—insufficiently?

What were we doing here now?

Compelled into these circumstances by A.D.'s dalliance, dissipation, despair and death. We had not come here to let our Philosopher discourage action but to act against the traitor in ourselves, to drive this couple from too easy an Eden. A tree-root uncovered, a pit lined with snow. . . . Hide them in a hollow? The murder-lust was again upon us.

A lizard zig-zagged like lightning in the crevices, making a home of rent earth, cleft places, fitting in wherever there was a parting.

We walked a good while down the mammoth mountain. Swallows skimmed along the low under-sky, plunging through the void—anchor-shaped swallows seeking anchorage.

We were no more than A.D.'s associates. Enlisted loyalty had made us partners in the same path. We had travelled towards each other; like unto like, echo unto echo, and a few ghosts to carry on the soul's fatigue. For we had come from far, and had yet far to go.

But we must first meet, embody in the One, settle our affairs. As the suicide of the head of the firm brings into active service the auxiliary, A.D., in a moment of inspiration, of vision, had called on and been heard by a sponsor, a counterpart, polarized, as each of us, with an affinity, a spiritual ally, what we are accustomed to consider our guardian angel.

And is not life but the vibration of the one towards that other?

Chapter XI

A MOUNTAIN STORM

LONG before nightfall there was a closing in, a compression; the air stood still awaiting a command. Heat lightnings split the horizon—or danger-signals of an approaching storm?

At a nearer thrust of lightning the round dark clouds rushed together, drumming in the thunder.

Flying columns assemble, livid as a rising of the dead.

The female land moaned and suffered to share in the reeling harsh passion of the wind.

High-crested trees, their roots ripping up the earth's edge, fell about us.

We rushed to the open field. Alarums of the released mad, the battle-cry of millions. In their midst an electric giant discharging luminous orders of destruction. An awakening death music, leading the heart into the thick of the fight under Gatling guns of rain.

Metallic rents, sky-quakers, a shattering and falling to pieces of the kingdom of light,—the heavy artillery cannoning at the other end, rumbling, changing its position, opening fire.

The impetus of a flash tore open vistas of a new day.

We ran, head downward, under stabs of steel, the taste of the storm grating between our teeth, our feet slipping without direction. Gullets gushing down the mountain-side, dancing with noise. Exchanging an unwieldy anger for an exultant power, we rose as the hurricane raged to a climax, and pulled the Glow-woman with us up through torrents of mud—the lightning lending us its phosphorescence, the thunder its might.

We steered for a golden glimmer seen at intervals. As we approached, the gold glimmer issued from a hut. We knocked. An old man unlatched and latched the door with difficulty, as we were let in to the thick warm smell of cows that were huddled together in the shed below.

In the room where we stood, high-lights played on huge copper cauldrons full of milk. In the next room about a dozen men were sitting on two benches, on either side of a lamp-lit table.

At an unusually loud crash, they would arrest the bread or wine-glass to cringe or look out.

A young shepherd, fleecy-headed as the lambs, hid his head in his arm each time the lightning entered through him.

The men tottered to their feet as the Glow-woman was revealed to them. Her dress, transparent with rain, singled out the well-known female secrets, as she stood against the small high window between the lamp and lightning.

They made place for her, and she sat down and ate of their bread and drank of their wine, for she was shivering and aglow and afright all at once.

We remained unobserved in the darker room, and drew ladles of milk to quench our thirst, from the nearest cauldron, watching the progress of the storm and the abated and renewed fright of the woman surrounded by lusty and half-drunken men.

The two on either side of her began touching her,—first as if to ascertain how damp her clothes still were; then without pretence, quite boldly.

As one put an arm around her, the other leant hard down on her, while the young shepherd stretching across the narrow table, rivetted her head by a kiss on the mouth.

The old man who had let us in growled:

"Leave her alone. We will all get into trouble. Can't you see they are hotel people? She and the storm will turn our milk."

But no one was ready to listen to him.

As an ultimate stroke, a purple quintessence, entered the hut, we seized the iron key from the door and hurled it, in a clap of thunder, straight at the lamp. It broke inaudibly in the greater crash and spread fire along the table.

In their disordered attempt to put out the fire and light another lamp, the Glow-woman, who had looked through the dark towards us for help, joined us at the door which we struggled to open.

As we did so, the rush of wind and rain was so strong she was thrown on the ground. In falling she hit the rim of one of the brass cauldrons and it chimed.

Some of the men, seeing her fall, hesitated whether to help her up or cover her.

"Shut the door, or you will squirt in the lightning. Plenty of thunder-bolts to go round. Bolt the door."

As this new warning diverted the attention, we both ran out.

Two of the men and the youth were seen against the outer side of the hut, determined to come after us, to have the woman who had refused them; but the rain beat down the blood from their excited faces and calmed their thick necks.

We had reached the mountain's ledge. Night was above, below and about us, and only by clinging to some brushwood could we keep our feet from the abyss.

The wind that never knows its own strong mind—the wind, in a paroxysm, drove the rain in bleating folds. Buttressed against the storm, the mountain reared its tidal-wave with the lighthouse on its top.

Taking the lead in love and danger—atavism of a dead chief—we asserted a last reserve of power, and compelled the Glow-woman, suffocating, exhausted, whipped by the rain, gagged by the wind, up to the summit, up the stairs of the turret, into our room.

In comparative safety, we took off our heavy clothing, nor minded the thunder, nor feared the lighting over which she tried to pull the curtains.

"We have not done with the storm, nor do we know how exhausted we are," she said, as she put a towel turban-wise around her drenched hair, and a match to the candles and the fire.

Sitting between the two chairs where our wrung clothes were hung to dry, panting as an athlete after a last round; and a trainer of her own body, she rubbed it down.

Topple her over into the fire to warm our heart towards her?

Remembering she had brought a bag, she got up and put on a nightgown, through which her body appeared as if X-rayed as she came near, holding out a night-shirt to us.

Intimacy, ignoble intimacy was webbing us in. Soon we should be sharing the same toilet utensils—

The wash-rag, with its peach smell,

The same bed-clothes.

Shameless shameful intimacy, with no ugliness left to hide, no beauty left to reveal.

Intimacy more obscuring than any separation,

Effacing all points of spiritual contact.

Slow devourer of the inner life,

Feeding daily on the vitals.

Two husks that lean one upon another, propped up by the give of each, a contribution to nothingness.

A colour passed over our eyes.

Things ominous, a shadow, might hasten between us.

The storm was still at daggers drawn. Their thrusts zig-zagged through the little mountain room. The lightning might serve:

Direct it through her flesh. Strike her down as a peace offering. The storm wanted a victim and so did we. A victim would justify and appease us.

We tried to seize the lightning and direct its hilt-less blades. We gave orders to the elements to do the work, but the elements would not obey our mortal command.

Our thwarted celestial authority turning us on earth into tyrants and fiends, we looked at her.

She could not stand our look, the violence of its electricity. Our nervous system diverging from two batteries sparked their full voltage from both our eyes.

She crouched—then straightening herself, she received the flash exultantly.

"How you can hate! You had not this concentration before, though you had, perhaps, greater cause to hate me. . . . No love has fired me as this new hate of yours. It may exterminate me, make me over . . . be creative of my death. I am so tired of desire—of desire without fulfilment. My beauty is sterile; it promises but does not keep its promises."

Then as tenderly, as tenaciously as a woman to her lover:

"Make me, kill me, take me, kill me."

Her hands held our hands tighter and tighter about her throat, her head had fallen back, her eyes revulsed. She wanted of us, and we of her, her death.

A sudden vision of what we were doing tore our hands off, leaving her death as we had left her joy uncompleted.

What right had she to die?

Would we be revenged indeed? Let live!

A lesser crime to kill than to let live?

She was not to join the "hidden people." We alone had that right.

We must keep her apart from them, from us. Draw the border-line and leave her on this side.

She was made for this surface world,— let her stay on it.

She still vainly prayed to us:

"Make me, kill me, take me, kill me!"

Running away from her, and the complicity she urged out of doors. The storm was spent, but drops sprinkled on our shoulders as a blessing from the roof we had just left. A kind of moisture, a poise of rain, fell with a gentle readjusted speed. Our nerves relaxed. Their grip on our fingers untightened, as we lifted our hands to the waters' baptising, making innocent our murderous fingers caught in the celestial strings, played upon by the rain-music, made on with the water-harps.

The thought of the women alone in the room beset us. She must go back to where she belonged. Had she not twice come too near the boundary of our dominion?

We would tell her of our, of A.D.'s promise to the dead woman, persuade her to let us leave her—go away.

The fear that she would, in some way, overtake us unless we reasoned her to sleep, made us tip-toe back. As gently as rain patters, we went upstairs.

She lay feverish in the child's bed. Though her features had fallen into the sleep harmony, tears still lustered between her joined lashes, straightening them down to her fire-flushed cheeks.

We set the child's bed rocking. As we bent over her a shower of raindrops fell from our hair into hers. She only turned, the lids of her breasts already full of forgetfulness.

Should we just go on rocking the child's bed where she slept? Or what sign should we leave to say we had returned before leaving?

How peacefully now she lay folded within herself.

The few wilted rose leaves of the rose she had given us, found in our coat pocket, we strew upon her:

"Farewell, farewell"—we doubled the word to make it doubly secure.

We move on feet standing within a dream,
Toward new paths, all pure;
We grope for clothes still warm as sleeping pets,
And strike the early riser's sulphurous match.
Our shadow, that the candle light throws out,
Escapes us through the window—
She-devil wavering on the nearest tree,
Naked and dispossessed, loosed on the night.
May the night catch and clothe the nakedness
    Of that defiant giant silhouette,
Shameless exaggeration of ourself!

Dark guide, nocturnal side and shape of us,
Now stretched before us, treading on our tread,
So joined and echoless we fear to crush
This figure cut out of our own reflection.
Decide who leads us—is it we, or you?
So we are cloaked and hooded in a hat?
How lose this artful costumed ape grotesque,
This ambler at our side that stains our steps,
Then runs before, a flighty thing on stilts,
    Black slave outpassing us?
How cut from us this shade-resembling self,
This form of death and dancing cypresses,
And so regain proportion and life-size?
We'll sell it for that money of the night,
    A poet's piece of silver.
There, too, we see a sombre effigy—
—Perhaps the mirrored shadow of our Love?
Rub out with softest clouds that woman's head,
Remint the moon to some new currency,
And pay the penalty of passing on.
    —On where? . . . The way? . . .
Into a reborn world so filmy new.
    And we the first one in it.
To change pale darkness for a harlequin,
Burn up our shadow in the rising sun,
Though the long twilights give it back to us.

CHAPTER XII

THE RETURN

THE LOVER and the Poet had extricated us from a situation where neither of them could serve.

On the mountain's edge, where we had wrestled with the storm, we sat wondering, in a clean-washed sky, over the survival of our fittest—over the bewildering interference of our own and other irresponsible personages.

That we might have been represented by our murderer or our sensualist, and become subject to actions involving us in their consequences, made us rejoice at our release.

The little town below, rocked by the storm, was at rest. No lights were in sight.

A quiet mist dropped at times its curtain. Clouds enveloped us, or broke away to drift up through the turret where the Glow-woman slept in the child's bed. She would awaken just as we left her, put out a hand, an arm, her arms to us; and the end would have to begin all over again. She was not read for us.

Those who are hardly anything have many lives to go. We could not advance her, or be set back.

Why did we allow ourselves to be misled?

As ever in such cases, we must blame the urge of a blind majority.

We were not yet governed by our higher representatives, though we had flashes of their growing power that might soon take up and shape events into their likeness.

If the legion could not hinder, we would disband the legion.

"Dominate rather than dispense with," argued our Economist, loath to part with anything.

A radiance came through the air . . . the morning star?

It approached with an unmistakable sound. An aeroplane had weathered the storm? Or was trying a round in the greying sky. It came so near that we recognized a bi-plane, seeking a table-land on which to alight. Two men were in it—her two?

They glimpsed the stretch beneath the summit, and having nosed an abrupt descent, climbed out.

Day was already diffuse enough for recognition, and Duthiers, on espying us, changed his course from the hotel—which the boy-husband quickly entered.

"You have evidently not accepted my pact," were Duthiers' first words, as he towered above us heavily booted and helmeted as a wingless man to the air.

"Shall we toss up to see who is to stay? Shall we toss up—or down, head down—whichever can throw the other over the edge? You have the advantage, as I am still dazed and unsteady after the strain of a rough flight. I am gallant enough to give you this handicap… or do you prefer to fly back with me? There should be as many ways out as into a false position. My letter suggested one way, but you do not seem to have agreed to it. So I've interrupted your elopement, and have actually brought about a most embarrassing situation. Shall I confess I revel in embarrassing situations; they alone smack of reality, make us inventive, prove our metal or its flaw! . . . So you won't fly back with me? Are you afraid? The value I place on my safety guarantees yours. The weather has quieted down; what wind there is left is travelling our way. We can get to Paris in a few hours . . . and I will install you in her flat and you can finish your days there going over your past, meeting in the spirit, and other enjoyable makeshifts. Aren't you anxious to refresh your love, to have all those letters in your possession at last?

"Break bread with me? If you don't put something in your stomach to steady it, it may leave you en route."

He bit into a sandwich as he handed some to us.

"Now, shall we drink to the return?"

He raised his flask from his side to our lips. We took a sip that ran a burning course through us. Then he drank, and we started to walk towards the bi-plane.

On coming up to it he stroked its varnished wings as though it were a successful racehorse.

Raising the flask he drank again, the apple Eve stuck in his throat registering his gulps, until it was empty, and its spirits became his.

He pointed to my place, then got into his and turned the spark-valve. The thing shook and palpitated. He registered the motor power, and began wheeling along to wrench away from the earth that seemed to attract the materials that had belonged to it. That wood and steel should fly propelled by mere machinery seemed inadmissible.

We brusquely severed from the ground into a gentle soaring. Steering on a low level right over the mountain's edge on a downward drop, we passed far above the town, by its lake, and below the cloud rifts. Though within touch, we could not say a word.

A new element scooped into the mouth, taking away our breath, filling the lungs to bursting, cutting up our throat.

Duthiers seemed well accustomed to such work—indeed, only at his best when coupled to a machine.

The cold became so intense that, feeling us shake, he indicated to aviator's stove, which we drew in our direction.

We dropped into thinner air that never was torn through, and readjusted our equilibrium much as a horse his fall and rise after jumping an obstacle.

Hurried through new dimensions, we had lost the sense of earthly speed and proportion. Was that vegetation a field of heather or a forest? Was that little agglomeration already Paris?

From where we sat we could not see the registering apparatus. Our faculties were dulled, our blood arrested like quicksilver in a broken thermometer. We felt none of our organs. All needs seemed for ever abolished.

We could have stood it indefinitely if it had not been for the noise, and the cold.

Should we never thaw?

Thoughts separated their ice and drifted down a stream of primitive consciousness:

> Intermediary
> analogies
> correlate
> energise
> reconciliation
> antithesis
> synthesis
> obedience
> consistency
> association
> emotional knowledge
> supreme occurrence:

to discover through the senses the communication. Meanings were forming around an exterior consciousness; then an awareness of self—a something sitting in space—situated itself.

The air-tide poured into our system, the opening dikes of memory carrying us on and away, as on the morning we rode forth and became each thing we looked upon, merged in universal receptivity:

> Wondrously suspended over an empty sea of air.
> The blonde disease of the wheat.
> The warm thick smell of the earth,
> Was that little agglomeration already Paris?

The two architectural monsters prepared to receive us—semi-circular sheds, masonic skeletons ribbed with rain-coloured glass, vaulted arches of the machine-god.

We swerved, sky-dizzy, getting on our land legs, our craniums still resounding with the trepidation.

Duthiers helped us down. Was the elastic fabric our food hardly touched the same sodden earth we had known?

Sunshine showered through us as we got into Duthiers' car.

Fresh from the sky without inscription, we learned to read all over again: "Octroi," "Porte d'Italie."

We pulled up by a church, a real little church. We had to bring ourselves back to its mediæval proportions, its garden with stone flowers that had fallen or been chipped from it. Matins chimed down from its belfry, and swinging doors let the faithful into the stained glass and candle-light moved by the chanting voices.

Duthiers led us to an abbey built right against the old church, and up the last flight to an apartment which he opened, before delivering the key to us.

He hesitated on the threshold that smelt of incense, then resolutely followed us into the antechamber.

"Aren't you afraid of me? There are other dangers left," he said, looking insinuatingly at us.

His words came to our ears, but no significance seemed attached to them. We heard as one from another world to whom the language of other regions is meaningless.

Yet we moved as accustomed to the room we had entered.—Memory, here is your port, we recognize these moorings!—

As a medium, our back aware of another presence, we went to the writing desk and discovered the hiding place of the letters.

Feeling ourselves seized by Duthiers, we looked at this primitive man as though ages separated us from him, and clairvoyant, as in a trance, we knew the grip meant a doubt whether after all we were not to have the better part, and an attempt at revenge at being kept out of the eternal feminine.

No provision of fear being found to apprehend danger, we became the onlookers of what was perhaps going to be our tragedy. As an Asiatic convict on whose drugged person torture is inflicted, we were aware of smiling back irrelevantly.

Duthiers tightened his grasp and shook us so violently that not only the package of letters we held, but the fan and letter in our pocket fell out.

We knelt to pick them up, but were pivoted round face to face, so close that through his eyes we saw into the mechanical workings of his instincts. His teeth bit a few inaudible injunctions.

Trying to master our unreality, he came even a step nearer. A brittle sound under foot made him look down: the dead woman's fan lay horribly crushed and menacing—a skeleton hand with mittened phalanges under his boot.

The superstition of a savage crept through his hard disciplined features as, dominated by an invisible enemy, he took his hands from our breast and stepped out the circle of relics. He gained the door, and shut it on his retreat.

As we picked up the broken fan, an air of past hours was wafted back to us. A sound of bracelets tinkled in mid-air . . . on the arm of the lost mistress, or just curtain rings moving in the breeze?

A door—not the one by which Duthiers went out (we heard that close reassuringly) opened hard by. Our heart fell out of place and thumped amongst the scattered letters . . . our heart, or was it the dead woman treading the floor?

—As gently as our thought of her, she enters. . . . Absence? . . . Silence?

Longing, the searchlight, shattered its long range against the walls to drop on little objects, magnifying them into importance.

We are so starved for her that we catch at anything to sustain us. Our love seems to have left no communication, until we discover her hidden signs; for those who exist in the spirit are more easily with us than those obscured by the flesh. They come more than half-way, but if we do not find their way they fade back upon themselves. How transcend this state of arrested development, touch the intangible, become also a spirit of free mingling—the survival of each in each to meet again? How rid ourselves of our burden, go to meet her? In regions of light, detect her radiance, her separate impalpable presence.

As we looked around, our first impression of intimacy reasserted itself. The house with a temple and this apartment set against a church, with voices echoing into a whisper of sacred music, had their analogies.

The childish ghost fright, or the ghost desire, had startled us?

All objects in the room bore a friendly relation to us and to one another. Crystal objects allowed but an interference of embellished light. It passed through an enormous block of rock crystal of so many different clarities that it scarcely outlined the rough contour against the free cubes of air contained in the half-shaded room. A halo of glass near the alcove opened directly into the church. As from a proscenium box, we looked through it, down into the fly-wings and on to the theatrical altar.

Though there were many indications that Stella had abandoned the religious practices of her ancestors, the pagan rites of Catholicism had accompanied her new life.

As the service progressed, the smell of incense increased; the great and small candles shone more partially on the chasubles of the priests than on the dim humbled backs of those kneeling. We stood outside the faith, above the dogmas, on a level with the stained glass angels transmitting the daylight through their translucent bodies and celestial attire, yet our need seemed the very breath of God.

Evolved from colour, cleansed in intrinsic values, in a love liberated from sensuous taint, we touched with reverence the relics that we had inherited: the clear witness of our love-life.

The clock had stopped as though to break with time that had so ill-used us. A crystal dagger's thick yet transparent hilt had once been encrusted with precious stones—a weapon to cut away the shadows of those who are but the living? A penholder and pen of glass—in one of its facets a tangle of colour, a play of prisms; an ink for thoughts of many hues?

There upon the floor lay, thick as autumn leaves, the trophies, the conquests of our sorrow, over which we reigned like lonely kings. As we bowed down to gather them together, a passage in the uppermost was as mind transference: "For surely to haunt is more than to possess!" And had not her fluid hand traced: "A lustral glitter rounds each object . . . we, too, will become as pliable as water to keep our place about you." . . .

And already how blended with the immaterial the whole letter:

I pass by the vanity of towns that reflect their image in the moving glass which does not carry on their images. They stay, in spite of the current, as fixed as the towns themselves.

On uninhabited rivers I glide, during this month of drought and separation from you. There was a time when it was as much separation as I could stand being no nearer than in your arms.

The banks have a scorched and vivified foliage, so varied that it replaces our coloured gardens. Far from the beaten roads, and between them, I rest from the fatigue others experience, and from all that is not myself: approaching all that pleads beautifully enough to become a part of me.

The River's philosophy: to glide so smoothly that its change seems to abide.

L'onde est un amant doux à qui sait le suivre
Son mol enseignement apprend comme il faut
    vivre.

From here everything matters and nothing matters—only rocked and somnolent realities reach me. They must traverse the water, be washed of their stains, mixed with reflections, reach the other shore.

Which of these trees is real? Both are real differently: that willow moved by the breeze, and that same willow which the water sways. Life and its reflections are equally real; that which I imagine happens as surely as that which happens.

Everything takes on a value and loses a value as seen from my houseboat's window at the level of the rivers that pass me as I pass.

Before her flowered bed of many silks (a fixed idea to the finger-tips—repeating the same rose over—obsession of just the selfsame rose, one same rose all the roses) we knelt before the rose, the absent rose.

And taking our armful of letters to her flowered bed, all the fire and tears that had gone to make them lay upon us, communicated directly to us the high, real, pure moments that are as life's apology.

Had we not gone farther than other couples in the surrender to desires that could not be satiated by any bodily gift? And even in joy, sharp tears had cut through our closed eyelids.

To punish our finite love, we invented gestures to destroy it. After the love-night and sleep together, A.D. would awaken the best beloved to shower words like poisoned arrows into her brain, distil in it ferments that would breed demons—and cast them out with the love that passes understanding.

The letters pieced out our whole spent liaison, and sometimes they recalled something of it, and sometimes we; and we were moved together and the white wings trembled in our hands as their soul soared out of them, or fell, as their bitterness broke again our broken love.

But the sweetness was the most persistent.

As bands round a mummy, they bound us, embalming us in their fragrance. Our thoughts went from each confessional: from the letters to the book. Had we not substanstiated, absolved and blessed A.D., and were we not ready now to be released?

"Ange pris dans ce charnel roman."

And while our tired body mused, drowsed and slept, an illumination came to us and touched us more perfectly than anything we had felt on earth.

And our arched ribs became a cathedral's flying buttresses, and our voice an organ, and our love a stoned angel.

Desire against desire, the battle of an imprisoned god. Our heart caught fire and burned as a sacred lamp within us, and the light shone through us that it might guide us to her. And our lover's arms stretched out to her, wider than the crucified arms of Christ: and we were joined together, and two lovers became one angel.

Chapter XIII

THE ONE TAKES LEAVE OF THE LEGION

AN explosion of sound, a roaring, a blotting of notes, a single blast, a summons to last judgment, a dreadful music: the organ, brought us to our feet, back to a consciousness conscious of its loss.

We had awakened from Paradise.

Its ecstasy had hardly faded from eyes that looked out on the neighbouring glass angels.

Day had taken away with it their seraphic colours, dependent on day for their splendour. Their negative attire remained outlined, held in place by a rim of lead.

While the One stood still resplendent, a sphere of separate air about the head, high above the legion, in angelic oneness, star distinct.

For the first time the One asserted:

I am I.

No longer receptive, but radiating, I escape from the Satanic plural, and its multiple conditions of existence. I escape with my single soul, incorporated in the light, indistinguishable, from the colours of the light.

The voices of nebulous galaxy, the voices of divergency and discord, the weighty misleading troop, questioned:

"How do you know that you exist without us?

"Are you so sure of finding us that you can give us up?

"How can you believe that there is anything else?"

"Because I am ready for it."

The choir of false representations continued:

"Your are the resolved Seventh . . . the sensitive note. . . .

"Our finest capacity vibrating beyond us, our supreme representative."

Our higher spirits urged:

"Gather all paths together, all reins in one hand.

"Many horses, a single way for the standing charioteer.

"Will you not lead us as we led you?

"Will you not say some essential things to us before we separate?

"Are there no essential things to be said—to guide us now that we stand apart?"

The body confronted the spirit with all those who had composed it—all but the low characters that had scampered off like rats from a doomed ship.

And they spoke in turn, or interrupted one another, subordinates serving their own ends, covering one another's voices, listening mostly to themselves, none listening to the silence of revelation about the One.

The Sensualist confessed:

"We hunger for some nourishment that is neither plenty nor abstinence.

"Give each their daily bread, you but shift the misery elsewhere.

"We starve in palaces, or our well-being puts us to sleep . . . and if we sleep, dreams are our scavengers.

"They break our substance and eat it in the gutter, and lap up our red wine.

"Prepare for us a feast that will satisfy."

The Senses emphasized:

"We are not much better than the average, though we have a beyond-sense that may rid us of the physical.

"Development is a natural expression of life, and as we cannot develop deeper into materiality, let us develop away from it.

"Teach us to sensitise the unseen, sniff what is in the wind—a cur's privilege.

"We are so obtuse that we could not even feel the presence of the Beloved until a higher medium joined us to her.

"Do not let us fall back where our sensations are but earthly reminiscences amongst those women with their escort of shadows.

"Save us from the grossness of our health, the false interpreter who puts a fresh circulation through us . . . From Desire, the hunter, who eggs us on to the same old chase."

The gusty hunter, and Health's companion, the rich blood, ran high in protestation:

"You cannot dispense with us; we give the beat, we start the movement.

"We quicken the game in the hypertrophied heart of the lover,—a full heart, a rose of many petals scattered about wildly—a heart rushed ahead, out of measure.

"No passion can exist without us.

"We are the emissaries of the heart.

"Our main-spring will not deny us."

The Heart:

"I am quartered like the Cross.

"A torrent of tears, a flood of fire, have cleansed me of your animal heat.

"You are a fluid of blindness full of humours as a charging bull.

"Does not our red magnificence give tone to all we invest?

"We would no longer see red—but see clear."

Insight, the Conqueror, and Discrimination, which is a bitter gift, were contradicted by Hope. Hope the human malady, from whose contagion most of the enlightened were immune.

Hope was supported by a voice that came from the dark vaults of the chest, breathing intoxication into words. It came from the Poet whose grey brain is reflective of the moon, of images and rhythms, of appearances, and sometimes of a fragment caught from the conversation of the gods. Surely the Poet might accompany ... was not of this world, hardly of this world.

The Philosopher argued against the Poet:

"The Poet who is always harping on death, must remain behind to write the epitaph, for the Poet's inseparable companion, the Lover, is also human. A graveyard is the last refuge of Romanticism . . . a poet's happy hunting-ground. To the philosopher graveyards are but laboratories of decomposition, of metamorphoses. . . . Absurd the cult of the living for dead bodies: the most unstable attached to the most changing.

"The Intelligence, our intelligence, alone is of a different extraction."

The Poet:

"The inspired intelligence, the feminine intelligence of the poet, the intelligence of intuition, of receptivity, may prove more valuable and prophetic than the philosophers' dogmatic ally, the protégé of wisdom

"And what is wisdom but amassed knowledge from the world of phenomena?"

The Philosopher:

"You take our name in vain. The inspired intelligence, the intelligence of the subconscious, you are so proud of, is but instinct—reappropriated memory, whereas our intelligence is a free agent independent, capable of abstract conclusions—highly mathematical."

The Poet:

"Here we meet and are blended. The higher mathematics become, *in extremis*, metaphysical. The spark that seizes the relationship, the go-between, the uniter, is not a part of the mortal brain, is therefore of divine essence.

"Art is a message from another world."

The Philosopher:

"Your speculations are presumptive, mine are based on exact Science. . . ."

The Poet:

"How many exact sciences have had to shift their position and acquiesce in some successful discovery of mine? I say discovery for want of a better world, for we only discover that which we know."

The Passions interrupted:

"Though both the intelligences you claim are good company, in an emergency we have found you of no help—our only salvation is to kill passions by finer passions.

"Your powers of seizing and transmitting are henceforth useless to one who enters each thing directly and detects its infinite correspondences.

"In vain you appeal to your old judge: a silent MIND, a mind gone its own way, a mind beyond remembering."

Then a shadow threw itself before the One, cut a last figure, an imploring shape on the floor, and swayed there in fear at no longer being in attendance.

The Black-Forces advanced behind it, former masters claiming a renegade, and so it was that our shadow became but the shadow of a shadow! . . . And all the prostrate shadows rose to make the evening.

The Philosopher, not allowing any dismissal, returned to argue, certain that in the mutiny which had broken out amongst the members of the legion, supporting and betraying one another through conviction, or to keep in favour, such a dominant intelligence would alone be preserved, for it could do its work on anything, anywhere:

"Why should not death be as habitable as these walls—the operating cells of the mind?

"A change of custom is not a disaster; dead, should we feel the line of demarcation, the difference?

"Death is but a certain degree of cold."

The Philosopher was interrupted by the most formidable opponents:

The Lover:

"I know death as no one living can know it. I, the Lover, who died for love!

"Before we give up our body to the nightmares that carried us to our birth and death, let us be absolved from the suicide. We have fulfilled the pledge to the book in the temple, taken up the mortal disguise, justified our part. Now liberate us from this convict prison, let the broad-arrow stigmata be effaced from the breast—the wound from the head. Let the connecting threads be broken, for they bind that which is healed.

"There is a love that would lead us out of all limits, as surely as there is a love that would destroy us in them. For love's sake let love forgive the erring lover. Forgive, too, the Lover's soul mistaken and deceived by circumstance, awakened in a net with the wrong mate, beating against its helplessness.

"With wings attending on the paths of sleep.

"Yet Love has saved the Lover, for love alone reinstates, is transmutable, of interchangeable value, to be taken wherever we go, through whatever we become.

"A metal melted in fire, minted in light, a white gold that no philosopher's stone can create. Our riches shall be estimated at how much of this wealth we contain and spend. Love alone shall determine our hierarchy in the kingdom to come. In the acceptance that is beyond affirmation, Love shall deny none that can stand its test. Nor does Love deny the great body which has possessed it and which it has possessed."

The breath of the organ moved the rose-embroidered bedspread; the music reaching through us uplifted the resonant box of the ribs, quivering spears through the impatient feet.

A detached soaring whirr, chased by a flight of vibrations, invaded the air; permeated, submerged, rolled under, dragged asunder in tides of intensified sound, trying to dissolve and win us to their motion, pushing us out, taking our place.

In a thud, a jumble of voices, overlapping, indistinct, sound-forms palpitated to blend. A stammering strength, a spiritual pressure, spirited us away. Our Presence, that concrete speck, dancing as it gets into our light?

We looked at our hands, through our hands, our bloodless shadowless hands, relieved from form and motion, folded within each other, at rest in the still centre of all movement, as immaterial as the crystal waving air, and hardly distinguishable from the crystal objects still about us.

In the half light half dark, we doubted our consistency. What had become of the flesh, the mortified fair soft skin that is so insensitive it cannot feel the touch of a spirit?

Obtuse Flesh, you do not know that "to haunt is greater that to possess"—go your way, leaving us to our transparency. The body, our hero, has yet a part to play.

It is the third day after death, the day of consummation.

It is the hour of the howling hound forgotten in the yard, the hour of the whinnying grey mare come to take back our knight-errant; a stirrup of pain binds the rider's feet! Re-lit the three candles of welcome.

Speed you well out of danger: dead! cured of convalescence, that delicately modulated study in degrees. The will to die is as powerful as the will to live. As the act of violence, of disintegration, had already been committed, you have only to ratify it. Remember who you are. Go back to answer for us, for yourself. Lie as a *gisant* on our lady's tomb; let the cold grey stone encompass you, your lips and features fade into its greyness. A stone knight, taken into the stone . . . hands petrified in prayer, as the cold reaches the heart.

Is not our dead heart already with the dead—with those living otherwise?

THE END

AUTHOR'S NOTE

FOR years I have been haunted by the idea that I should orchestrate those inner voices which sometimes speak to us in unison, and so compose a novel, not so much with the people about us, as with those within ourselves, for have we not several selves and cannot a story arise from their conflicts and harmonies?

Let us seize the significance of life where it is unique, not where it is repetitive. Our thoughts more than our actions represent us.

Let us report from their live-centres.

A new star makes a new heaven.

Have not material things a spiritual double, and have we not met, in moments of inspirations, of heroism, a force that surpasses us? Its presence is in the works of genius. It is only when we surpass ourselves that we exist.

In our human composite, part ape and part angel, is there not scope for an extreme realism and spirituality? And might not an Epicurean be defined as a "Fourth-dimensional Materialist"? In the last sense materiality becomes spiritual, whereas spirits may take human shape. Mystery remains the invisible link between what is outworn by knowledge, and the unborn reality.

For those who would have our obscurities brought into opera-glass focus shall we, as in the theatre, condense our argument?

A.D., a being having committed suicide, is replaced by a sponsor, who carries on the broken life, with all the human feelings assumed with the flesh, until, having endured to the end in A.D.'s stead, the composite or legion is disbanded by the One, who remains supreme.

DRAMATIS PERSONÆ.

A.D. Self-destructive. A lover.

THE ONE. A.D.'s angel come to live in A.D.'s stead

THE GLOW-WOMAN. A beauty of the flesh that we have only met in the flesh.

STELLA. A beauty of the spirit that we have met in many ways, and loved and lost, and loved and found again in loving.

DUTHIERS. A third person in all situations.

THE BOY-HUSBAND who only exists through others.

A SHADOW WITHOUT A MASTER.

A.D.'s HORSE.

THE LEGION. Low characters, spirits—a hierarchy of selves.

TIME. Beyond time.